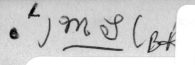

D0724156

Adopt-A-Book
Your library. Your Success.

Purchase of this book
was made possible by

Warren Jollimore

October - December 2012

1972 - 2012
Celebrating
40
years

South Shore
Public Libraries

TRC

DON'T MISS THESE
ALL-ACTION WESTERN SERIES
FROM THE BERKLEY PUBLISHING GROUP

THE GUNSMITH by J. R. Roberts

Clint Adams was a legend among lawmen, outlaws, and ladies. They called him . . . the Gunsmith.

LONGARM by Tabor Evans

The popular long-running series about Deputy U.S. Marshal Custis Long—his life, his loves, his fight for justice.

SLOCUM by Jake Logan

Today's longest-running action Western. John Slocum rides a deadly trail of hot blood and cold steel.

BUSHWHACKERS by B. J. Lanagan

An action-packed series by the creators of Longarm! The rousing adventures of the most brutal gang of cutthroats ever assembled—Quantrill's Raiders.

DIAMONDBACK by Guy Brewer

Dex Yancey is Diamondback, a Southern gentleman turned con man when his brother cheats him out of the family fortune. Ladies love him. Gamblers hate him. But nobody pulls one over on Dex . . .

WILDGUN by Jack Hanson

The blazing adventures of mountain man Will Barlow—from the creators of Longarm!

TEXAS TRACKER by Tom Calhoun

J.T. Law: the most relentless—and dangerous—manhunter in all Texas. Where sheriffs and posses fail, he's the best man to bring in the most vicious outlaws—for a price.

JAKE LOGAN

SLOCUM
AND THE
TEXAS TWISTER

JOVE BOOKS, NEW YORK

THE BERKLEY PUBLISHING GROUP
Published by the Penguin Group
Penguin Group (USA) Inc.
375 Hudson Street, New York, New York 10014, USA
Penguin Group (Canada), 90 Eglinton Avenue East, Suite 700, Toronto, Ontario M4P 2Y3, Canada
(a division of Pearson Penguin Canada Inc.) • Penguin Books Ltd., 80 Strand, London WC2R 0RL,
England • Penguin Group Ireland, 25 St. Stephen's Green, Dublin 2, Ireland (a division of Penguin
Books Ltd.) • Penguin Group (Australia), 250 Camberwell Road, Camberwell, Victoria 3124, Australia
(a division of Pearson Australia Group Pty. Ltd.) • Penguin Books India Pvt. Ltd., 11 Community
Centre, Panchsheel Park, New Delhi—110 017, India • Penguin Group (NZ), 67 Apollo Drive,
Rosedale, Auckland 0632, New Zealand (a division of Pearson New Zealand Ltd.) • Penguin Books
(South Africa) (Pty.) Ltd., 24 Sturdee Avenue, Rosebank, Johannesburg 2196, South Africa

Penguin Books Ltd., Registered Offices: 80 Strand, London WC2R 0RL, England

This is a work of fiction. Names, characters, places, and incidents either are the product of the author's
imagination or are used fictitiously, and any resemblance to actual persons, living or dead, business
establishments, events, or locales is entirely coincidental.

SLOCUM AND THE TEXAS TWISTER

A Jove Book / published by arrangement with the author

PUBLISHING HISTORY
Jove edition / October 2012

Copyright © 2012 by Penguin Group (USA) Inc.
Cover illustration by Sergio Giovine.

All rights reserved.
No part of this book may be reproduced, scanned, or distributed in any printed or
electronic form without permission. Please do not participate in or encourage piracy of
copyrighted materials in violation of the author's rights. Purchase only authorized editions.
For information, address: The Berkley Publishing Group,
a division of Penguin Group (USA) Inc.,
375 Hudson Street, New York, New York 10014.

ISBN: 978-0-515-15113-8

JOVE®
Jove Books are published by The Berkley Publishing Group,
a division of Penguin Group (USA) Inc.,
375 Hudson Street, New York, New York 10014.
JOVE® is a registered trademark of Penguin Group (USA) Inc.
The "J" design is a trademark of Penguin Group (USA) Inc.

PRINTED IN THE UNITED STATES OF AMERICA

10 9 8 7 6 5 4 3 2 1

If you purchased this book without a cover, you should be aware that this book is
stolen property. It was reported as "unsold and destroyed" to the publisher, and neither the
author nor the publisher has received any payment for this "stripped book."

ALWAYS LEARNING   **PEARSON**

1

"Stop! You gotta stop or we're gonna be killed!"

John Slocum didn't bother looking back down into the stagecoach compartment. The man had been raising holy hell ever since they had left Buena Vista on the Pecos River and headed for the town of Gregory, a couple miles outside of Fort Stockton. West Texas was never easy to travel in. Today was worse than the day before, and it looked to be getting nastier by the minute.

Slocum looked up at the clouds coming lower as if to crush him. They showed him leaden bottoms and were beginning to swirl in ominous patterns. He had seen a tornado or two in his day, and if anyone would bet him, he'd lay heavy money on these clouds spawning a twister. Soon. The coloration was turning a corroded copper green mixed with the darkness. That didn't always mean a dangerous tornado, but meant the road to Gregory was going to be an uneasy one.

"Got to keep moving," he yelled in reply. More than the worrisome weather, he hated riding alone in the driver's box. His shotgun messenger, Curly Will Beatty, had taken ill and had been in so much pain he couldn't make the trip. Curly Will was so thin he disappeared if he turned sideways. His scraggly beard never changed from month to month, remaining a tangle of black wire infested with bugs Slocum couldn't put a name to. But Curly Will had eyes so sharp he could make out a rider on the horizon five minutes before Slocum spotted him. More than once in the past three months the shotgun guard had saved them from being robbed.

"The damned wheel's fallin' off! We're gonna die out here if you don't do somethin!"

Slocum tried to ignore the passenger's strident complaint. He had driven this route often enough to learn every bump and pothole in the road. While it might be a stretch boasting he could drive it blindfolded, it wouldn't be far wrong. The last fifteen miles into Gregory were easy in that they were rolling hills and prairie going into desert. The road was sunbaked and in good shape, but not if the rains came pelting down on it.

A wobbly wheel in mud would likely delay them longer than taking care of it now.

But Slocum wanted to get to Gregory fast this trip, complaining passenger be damned. Not having Curly Will with him wore heavily on him since there was a huge payroll for the soldiers at Fort Stockton tucked away in the boot. The iron box carried the strongest padlock Slocum had ever seen, and the whole shebang had been bolted to a large brass plate that weighed as much as he did. Nobody was going to waltz off with it and not know they had done some real work.

That worried Slocum even more. Road agents were more likely to kill the driver and passengers and take their time blowing off the lock rather than simply making off with the strongbox. He had a cynical bent and figured this was exactly what the bosses at Butterfield Stage Company intended. Better to lose a driver and a few passengers than that damned Army payroll.

"The wheel! The wheel's comin' off!"

Slocum slowed, bent far to his left, and took a gander at the rear wheel. He cursed under his breath. Loudmouthed passengers irritated him. He got even madder when they were right. If he drove another mile, he'd lose that wheel. Pulling hard on the reins, he slowed the team and finally brought them to a halt. Fastening the reins around the brake, Slocum vaulted out and landed hard beside the coach.

"You finally got some sense jolted into your pea brain?"

"I'm looking at it," Slocum said. For two cents he'd knock the man's store-bought teeth down his throat.

"Don't take too long gettin' it fixed," piped up another passenger. The third remained quiet.

"I got my eye on the clouds," Slocum assured the man. He was as annoying as Loudmouth, but in a different way. He had a know-it-all attitude that galled as much as the strident complaints about the stagecoach's condition.

"Well that you should. Mark my words, we got a twister coming," the man said pompously.

Slocum almost wished the sky would clear, just to shut the man up and put him in his place. That wasn't likely to happen. As he went to examine the loose wheel, a drop of rain splatted against his hat brim and dripped off as he bent to examine the wheel. Hand against the rim, he pushed hard enough to rattle the wheel and show the problem. The hub nut had shaken loose over the rough road a few miles back.

He walked to the rear of the stagecoach and raised the canvas flap over the boot. The bright brass plate with the strongbox bolted on to it mocked him. Its weight might have caused the wheel to come loose since all the passengers' luggage had been tied down on the top of the stage. He poked around and found a small ax, then stalked off the road with it clutched in his hand until his knuckles turned white.

"Where the hell you goin'? This ain't no time to take a leak!"

Slocum called back, "Climb on out of the stage. We're all going to have to work to get the wheel snugged up again."

The trio grumbled. Loudmouth climbed out, followed by Know-it-all. The third passenger joined them, whispering. Slocum didn't have to overhear to know he was badmouthing not only the stagecoach company but the driver and about everything else. Loudmouth, Know-it-all, Complainer. Or maybe an instigator without the nerve to be open about it.

Slocum took out his frustration on the largest limb on a cottonwood tree that he could reach, chips flying with every swing. He imagined those chips to be the body parts of the three passengers in turn. He finally cut down a limb as thick as his arm, then chopped off its smaller branches and dragged it back to the road.

"Get a couple big rocks and put them under the axle."

"It's your job to fix the stage, not ours." The Know-it-all was medium height, wore a bowler turned brown from dust and a coat that had seen better days. The man, in spite of his shabby clothing, held himself like he was superior in all ways.

"Then I'll jump on one of the horses from the team, ride on into Gregory, get help, and come back for you. Can't say how long that might take." Slocum glanced significantly at the sky. The storm clouds were moving faster, lower, and the greenish tinge was more pronounced.

"You can't leave us out here! Not in this weather!"

As if to emphasize the problem, a large raindrop hit the top of the man's bowler and bounced a few inches, sending spray onto the other two passengers. They flinched and angrily began arguing. At least Slocum didn't have any reason to listen. He dragged the sturdy tree limb behind the stage, dropped to his knees, and began moving large rocks to block the right rear wheel. Then he turned his attention to putting a pile of rocks directly under the axle to use as a base for the lever.

Shoving the limb into place, Slocum adjusted the rocks. He stood, applied a little weight to the end of the lever, and saw that the stage would lift far enough for him to work on the wheel nut. The leather straps acting as springs creaked as he leaned down a bit more, then released the lever.

"You gents done jawing? A couple of you can lift the stage while I work to get the nut tightened. Or do you want to sit out here in the rain?"

A few more gravid drops splatted against the stage to add energy to the men coming to his aid. He pointed. Loud-mouth and Complainer put their backs to the lever while Know-it-all joined Slocum.

"You hold the wheel in place while I whack at the tightening nut," Slocum said.

"Be sure to use the hammer on the back of the ax head. Otherwise, you'll damage it further."

Slocum glared at the man, then bellowed to the other two passengers to lift. The stage came off the ground and let the loose wheel flop back and forth. Know-it-all knew enough to hold it in place as Slocum hammered at the nut to tighten it. He saw that the nut actually went back into place. He had feared the axle was damaged or the nut itself cracked so that it would break. After a few strong whacks, Know-it-all shook the wheel. Solid. It didn't wobble one little bit. Slocum saw how this bothered Complainer, who looked around from the rear of the stage.

"Lower the stage," Slocum said, stepping back to watch as weight returned to the wheel. It needed more work than he could give out here in this desolate landscape but they weren't more than a few hours outside Gregory. The stage company could get a wheelwright to do a decent—permanent—job.

"It won't last long," Know-it-all said. "I've seen such repairs fail within a mile."

"Get in. We'll drive until it falls off," Slocum said. "Less you don't have sense enough to get out of the rain."

No more drops fell but a touch of wind was whipping across the prairie to give warning of real storms to follow.

"Don't say I didn't tell you," the man said, giving the wheel one last shake. It didn't budge.

Slocum ignored him and the other two as he climbed up into the driver's box. Worrying about tornadoes and road agents suited him better than dealing with the passengers and their foibles. He pulled the reins from the brake, made sure it was released, then snapped the reins to get the team pulling. He heard a yelp of surprise. One of them hadn't clambered into the compartment fast enough. Slocum didn't give a good goddamn.

He took a quick look back to be certain the wheel no longer wobbled. It hit a pothole and didn't show any sign of coming off. He settled back onto the hard bench seat and squinted as he looked ahead along the road. Clouds moved with disturbing speed at such a low height he thought he could reach up and touch them. The greenish tinge was stronger now and the circular movement along with it. Tendrils of gray cloud dipped down in the distance, wisps hardly thicker than fog—but a warning. This was how a tornado looked before it touched down.

A sudden gust of wind grabbed at his hat, forcing Slocum to pull the brim down lower on his forehead. But he looked up quickly when something didn't feel right to him. Again he cursed not having Curly Will beside him. The scarecrow of a man would have spotted the rocks in the road instantly.

Slocum shoved his feet down into the footrest and pulled hard enough on the reins to put strain across his shoulders. The team had just gotten to speed and slowing them so soon was a chore. He finally brought the team to a slow walk, giving him a better chance to study the rocks in the road.

No way were they stretched across like a low wall from any natural cause. The only reason to block the road this way was that outlaws lurked. Slocum stopped the stagecoach and reached for his rifle just as Loudmouth shouted his displeasure at stopping again.

He poked his head out a window on the right side of the

stage to berate Slocum just as the first bullet tore splinters from the door. Yelling incoherently, Loudmouth ducked back. Slocum hiked the rifle to his shoulder and hunted for the shooter.

Someone had gone to a great deal of effort to block the stagecoach on the road, but then hid and did not try to advance to rob the payroll after a single warning shot.

Slocum was sure road agents were after the payroll. He had a few mail bags, too, tucked alongside the strongbox, but the Fort Stockton payroll had to be the plum waiting for plucking.

He scanned the area where the shot had come from but saw no movement. Although it was early afternoon, it might as well have been sundown. The heavy clouds cut off most of the sunlight and turned the landscape into ever-shifting gray shadows that caused him to jerk this way and that as he hunted for an outlaw to shoot.

"We gotta get out of here!" Whoever had made the order sound shrill and bordering on hysterical didn't understand the situation.

Slocum had no time to point out that the barricade in the road kept them from driving on, and the deep gullies on either side of the road prevented him from avoiding the rock wall without overturning the stage. He crawled on top of the stage and flopped on his belly, curling around the pile of luggage and using it for cover. Nowhere did he see so much as a hint of the gunman.

"You need help, driver?"

Slocum recognized Loudmouth.

"Stay inside. Can't find the robber." Slocum made another visual sweep of the horizon, not for the first time wishing Curly Will were there. Not only was the guard sharp of eye, he was also as accurate as anyone Slocum had ever seen at a hundred yards. Slocum was no tyro himself. He had spent a part of the war as a sniper for the CSA, sitting in a tree crotch all day, not moving, never betraying his presence as he waited for the Yankees to form their attack lines. The bright flash of sun off golden braid meant an officer harangued his troops. A single shot often robbed the enemy of its commander. Slocum couldn't claim he had won any battles because of his expert sharpshooting, but more often than not those fights had gone the way of the Rebs.

He was patient but nothing moved except the increasingly ominous swirling clouds overhead. They had scudded low before. Now he felt the hairs on the back of his neck prickling up. That was never a good sign. A lightning storm was the least of his worries with the rapid spinning in the clouds pulling down several funnels.

"We ain't gettin' our asses shot off in here!"

Slocum heard the door creak open on the stage. He started to warn the trio back inside, then decided this might provoke the road agent lying doggo somewhere out on the prairie. The rolling hills hid too much. The sparse vegetation came from too little rainfall over the course of a year, and the movement of the occasional leaf or thorny limb came from raindrops rather than road agents.

"Where are they? I'll take care of those yellowbellies."

Slocum didn't have to look to see who had spoken. It had to be Know-it-all. The arrogance in his words was his doom.

A single shot rang out. Slocum jerked around, saw where the sniper had hidden, and began firing methodically into the clump of waist-high grass. Slug after slug tore off pieces of the grass but no return fire sounded.

This was the damnedest robbery Slocum had ever seen—and he had been on both sides, being robbed and doing the robbing.

"They shot him. H-He's dead! He's stone-cold dead!"

Slocum wiggled forward and looked over the edge of the stage. Know-it-all lay sprawled on his face, his six-shooter dropped a few inches from his limp fingers. From the distance, the robber was either one hell of a fine shot or had been lucky. For Know-it-all, the matter was moot.

"I might have chased off the robbers," Slocum said. He doubted that but wanted to keep his surviving passengers calm. With as much gold as there was likely tucked away into that massive strongbox in the stagecoach boot, robbers weren't going to kill one man and leave. They'd see the death as one less man to keep them from getting filthy rich at the Army's expense.

"Then let's get the hell out of here!" That was Loudmouth blubbering like a baby.

"Can't drive around the barricade they threw up. You go and clear the road. I'll stand guard."

"Like hell you will! I ain't budgin'. I seen what happened to *him*!"

"One of you come on up here and keep watch, then," Slocum said. It surprised him when Complainer scrambled to the top and sat cross-legged atop the luggage.

"All I got's a derringer," he said. Slocum silently passed him the rifle. The man took it and appeared to know which end to point toward the road agents.

As satisfied as he could be by this, Slocum slithered over the side of the stage and dropped to the ground, the bulk of the compartment between him and where he had shot up the clump of grass. Over the years he had developed a feel for when he killed a man and when he had missed. His bullets hadn't even winged the varmint out there on the prairie causing such woe.

He touched the Colt Navy slung in its cross-draw holster to assure himself he could fire back if necessary, then hiked to the stone wall. It had taken some time to construct the barricade, and it took Slocum longer than he liked tossing the middle of it to one side of the road or the other in a gate wide enough to drive through. With every rock he heaved away, he tensed, sure a bullet would rob him of life as it had Know-it-all. He finished and hastened back to the stagecoach.

"Ain't seen nobody movin' out there. If Fred hadn't got hisself kilt, I'd have thought we were out here all alone."

"Fred's his name? What's his whole name?"

"Cain't say. We passed a flask around and got a bit friendly, but only a bit. First names and nothing more. He didn't think much of my whiskey, but what the hell? Sorry now I wasted a drop on him."

"He won't have anything more to feel all superior to," Slocum said.

"Wasted the whiskey, I did. And he even spilled more 'n I drunk."

The complaints continued as the man settled down in the driver's box, still clinging to the rifle as if his life depended on it.

"You going to ride with me? As guard?"

"You got to drive fast. I ain't gonna get wet sittin' here forever. Seat's not much better 'n inside either."

The man's complaining never stopped as Slocum worked the team up to a slow walk, passed the rocks, and then had nothing but empty road ahead. He craned his neck around occasionally, hunting for the gunman who had killed one of his passengers, then had just run off. It didn't make sense a road agent getting spooked so easily after the careful planning and physical work that had gone into staging the robbery.

"How far are we from town?"

"Maybe five miles from Gregory and another three from Fort Stockton," Slocum said. "If the team doesn't falter, we can make Gregory within the hour."

"Damned good thing. Rain's gettin' harder." Complainer wiped water from his face with a strangely delicate touch of his fingertip and left brown, muddy streaks on his cheeks. He looked like a Comanche on the warpath. "I'm gonna drown if I stay in this here box much longer. Stop the coach so's I kin get back inside. Them canvas flaps won't keep out much water, but it'll be better than gettin' drenched up here."

Slocum felt the strain across his back as he pulled the team to a halt to let Complainer join Loudmouth in the

surroundings. The roar in his ears died down to a muted hum. Under his slicker he was aware that he was soaked clean through and that his clothing had been cut to shreds like the heavy canvas that had protected him. A bit of fumbling reassured him that his six-shooter was still in its holster. The leather thong over the hammer had kept it from flying away when he had spun through the air.

"The twister!" Details snapped back into focus for him. He had been in the driver's box when the tornado picked up the stage and flipped it ass over teakettle. He had been flung from the box and had gone his separate way.

A troubling memory of seeing the horses caught in the tornado and carried aloft made him shudder. They had remained bridled together as the whirling wind had taken them away. How long they could have survived was anyone's guess. Slocum doubted it had been too long. He looked around, getting his bearings. A few nearby planks of painted wood were all that remained of the stage.

"Hallo!" His cry was smothered by the wind. He stepped over the ditch running almost bank to bank with rain and found the roadbed. Only the direction of the wind gave him any hint as to where he was. The darkness wasn't complete, but with the sheets of rain falling all around, it might as well have been.

It was the wind that told him which way to walk along the road. The twister had come up from behind. The wind had been blowing toward Gregory. He pulled the brim of his hat down and trudged along in the mud, stepping over bits of the sundered stage.

Less than a hundred yards toward the town, he heard a faint cry for help. At first Slocum thought it might only be his imagination, then the plea came louder.

"Here. Over here. To your right. Help me, for the love of God, help me!"

The ditch alongside the road ran wider here with the storm water, forcing Slocum to vault over it. He had most of his strength back but still almost fell into the small river, dropping to his knees to keep from being swept away. Even an inch of rapidly flowing water could knock a man from his feet. The water here would have been over boot tops.

"Driver, I need help. Please!"

Slocum saw a hand waving feebly through the rain and homed in on it, though it vanished now and then, dropping to the ground. He topped a small rise and saw Complainer flat on the ground. It had taken most of the man's strength to call out and lift his arm. Slocum dropped down beside him.

"How bad you hurt?"

"Can't say. Hurt all over. Feel like I been rolled around inside a drum, then got beat on."

Slocum had the man lift his arms and straighten his legs, then checked to be sure nothing important had been broken by the twister.

"You look to be in one piece."

"Glory be, how's that possible when I hurt like this?"

"Tornadoes are strange critters," Slocum said. "They can destroy the strongest building but leave a flower blooming beside it. Me and you, we got lucky. Can you stand?"

Slocum helped him to his feet. It took several tries before the man could walk with Slocum's arm around his shoulders for added support. They got back to the road. It was necessary to check the wind's direction again because Slocum had gotten turned around. That warned him he wasn't as sharp as he had thought before.

"I can't make it into town. That's miles."

"I can leave you and fetch help, but the tornado went this way. If it hit Gregory, there might not be a whole lot of folks able to come back for you."

"Don't leave me. I'll keep up. I will."

They walked in silence for the better part of an hour. Slocum glanced at the man, who had been complaining the whole way until the funnel cloud had snatched them from the stagecoach. The experience had mellowed him and put a cork in his nonstop griping.

"Dizzy, hard to stand up," the man said.

"Let's set for a spell," Slocum said. He needed to rest, too. There wasn't a muscle in his body that didn't feel as if he had just lost a hundred-round bare knuckles fight.

"What's your name?" Slocum didn't tell him he had his own cognomen already thought up.

"Rafael Stanton. Friends call me Rafe." The man lifted his chin and studied Slocum. "Don't know you'd want me for a friend, or me you, but you can call me Rafe or whatever else you want, for all that."

Slocum had to laugh at that. He introduced himself.

"Mr. Slocum, you have a knack for surviving. Out here in this miserable West Texas desert, that's the only thing to have. I'm glad you was drivin'."

"You a newcomer?"

"I'm on my way to Fort Davis. Bought half share in a store there from my brother. He's the only family I got left." Stanton coughed, then spat. "Fact is, he's the only one who'll put up with me."

"There are things to be thankful for in the world. And what you can't change, you might just live with."

"You noticed my constant complainin'?" He shook his head, and blood mixed with rain flew off in tiny droplets. "Wife said that, too, 'fore she upped and died. Cancer, the doctor said. Might just have been she reached the end of her rope puttin' up with me."

"A man can change," Slocum said.

"After comin' this close to death, I got reason enough. No amount of complainin' would call off that damned tornado."

"Let's get back to the trip. We're almost there."

And he was right. Less than a half hour later, the town of Gregory showed in front of them. Or what was left it. The twister had dashed about every other building, taking out those on the right side of the street while leaving those on the left. From what Slocum could see as he trudged in, most of the glass windows along the south side of the street weren't even broken. He might have thought a vandal had knocked out the few broken windows.

Doing an about-face to see what remained on the other side of the street would have convinced him it hadn't been a vandal but an army of outlaws as thorough and vindictive as any of Quantrill's Raiders during the war. Utter devastation had leveled the buildings and left only rubble.

"The hotel might have been leveled," Stanton said, "but the saloon's still running." The man shuffled off, balance precarious. He caught himself on the saloon wall, then spun around and stumbled inside.

Slocum considered following him. He was hungry and needed a shot or two of even cheap trade whiskey to kill some of the aches and pains he had accumulated on the trip from Buena Vista. But duty pressed down on his shoulders. The stage office was on the intact side of the street and the door stood ajar, people moving about inside the depot. Reporting the situation to the stationmaster mattered more than the rotgut he was likely to pour down his gullet.

For the moment.

He pushed the depot door open all the way to see the portly stationmaster sitting behind a cluttered desk. Henry Underwood looked up, then did a double take when he realized Slocum stood in the doorway.

"Land o' Goshen," Underwood said. "Get the man a chair." This he directed to a youngster who looked like he had been pulled through a knothole backward.

The boy's hair was in wild disarray and his clothing as ripped as Slocum's. It didn't take much guesswork to figure the boy was another survivor of the tornado that had struck Gregory.

Slocum sank into the chair, aware for the first time how bone tired he was.

"I didn't hear you drive in. You got . . ." Underwood's voice trailed off. "What happened, Slocum? Where's the stagecoach?"

"Gone, smashed to splinters by the tornado. I was lucky to get away alive." He described how he had been thrown high into the air but wasn't carried away by the cyclonic storm the way the team had.

"You lost the passengers?" Underwood spoke carefully, but Slocum knew the stationmaster's real question was hanging on the tip of his tongue.

"Came in with one, one's dead being shot down by the road agents, and the third?" He shrugged his shoulders. Even this small motion hurt like hell.

Underwood started to ask the question. Slocum beat him to it.

"The payroll's gone. Blown away. The tornado took it along with the rest of the stage."

"Dear Lord," the stationmaster said, collapsing in on himself. "We got to tell the Army right away. They might send out a patrol to hunt for it."

"The same twister that got me hit Gregory," Slocum said. "Any luck finding the townspeople carried off by the wind?"

"People ain't gold," Underwood said positively. "We got a chance of getting the payroll back. I got a telegram telling how the shipment was bolted to a brass plate weighing over two hundred pounds. With the strongbox and payroll gold, it was heavier than four hundred."

"Doesn't make a difference to a twister," Slocum said. "I thought I heard a freight train roaring down on me. It was the wind. The damn thing spun so fast it blurred my vision. There's no way to stand against such power."

"Gregory will rebuild. New folks will come in. If we can replace the stagecoach, they'll come on the stage and by wagons. This is a good place, sweet water in the wells, Fort Stockton not so far away to protect us from Apaches and the rest of them Injuns." Underwood took a deep breath. "You got to report the loss right away."

Slocum looked hard at the stationmaster. Telling an Army officer his payroll was missing might get him hanged on the spot. Or maybe they wouldn't wait to build a gallows. A firing squad would do just fine.

"That's your job."

"Yours," Underwood insisted. "Don't fret none. They ain't gonna harm you. Killin' the messenger what brings bad news isn't what they do over at the fort." He coughed behind his hand, then looked up to see if Slocum was buying his lie. "They got to keep you alive to recover their money."

"There's no telling where it ended up," Slocum said. "For the twister to carry away a couple hundred pounds of dead weight was nothing. That strongbox might be miles from here."

"Git yerself on over there, Slocum. Take a horse. Not the stallion. That one's mine. Take the gelding paint. He's sturdy enough to git you there an' back, even if he's seen better days."

Argument would get him nowhere, so Slocum went to the corral behind the stage depot and found the paint nervously pawing at the ground. Why it hadn't bolted and run off when the tornado hit was anyone's guess. Maybe it had and Underwood had retrieved it. That was unlikely, but Slocum was seeing a powerful lot of things he couldn't understand. After saddling, he stepped up and started the horse walking slowly in the direction of the fort.

In spite of the stationmaster's soothing words, he expected to be received like some kind of criminal.

He wasn't far wrong.

3

"Sergeant, throw this man in the stockade!" Captain Legrange's handsome face turned beet red from anger. "If he resists, shoot him. Hell, if he resists, call me and *I'll* shoot him!"

The enlisted man looked at Slocum and obviously would have preferred kissing a rattlesnake to taking away Slocum's six-shooter before putting him into the stockade.

"Can I get a couple men to help, Captain?"

"Forget it," Legrange said, grinding his teeth together. The ruddiness faded from his face as he got a better hold of his emotions. "There's got to be some way of recovering our payroll."

"Send for another, sir," the sergeant said. He sucked in his gut and stared straight ahead, coming to attention when the captain's ire turned toward him.

"It would take a month and a ton of paperwork. We'll get next month's payroll before we see replacement for this month's."

"Sir!" The sergeant braced himself. "What should I do

with him?" The man's eyes darted in Slocum's direction, then snapped back straight in front of him.

Captain Legrange began chewing on his lower lip as he thought. Slocum considered letting the man stew until he came to his own conclusion, but that might not work out too well. He might lash out again at the man bringing the bad news.

"I know you're spread mighty thin, Captain," Slocum said, "what with the tornado destroying half of Gregory the way it did." He looked around. Fort Stockton had escaped the ravages of the twister, except for hailstone damage and torrential downpour, but most of the company had been sent to find survivors across the countryside.

"What's your point?"

"Might be we can find the box, if we hunt for it." Slocum shrugged. "But you know how unpredictable a twister is."

"Sergeant, has Major Conrad returned yet?"

"Still on patrol, sir."

Legrange cursed and chewed some more on his lip. Slocum wondered if the chow was that bad at the fort for the officer to seek a new source of fresh meat. That brought a small smile to his visage, and the angry officer saw it immediately.

"What's so funny, Slocum?"

"There a reward for finding the payroll?"

"You're an employee of the stage company. You're getting paid already."

Slocum held his tongue. He wasn't being paid because there was no stagecoach to drive. Until a new one was built or driven in from Fort Worth to Buena Vista and finally to Gregory, he was unemployed. Not for the first time since reaching Fort Stockton, he thought about just riding on. Let Underwood swear out charges against him for horse stealing, since the tired old paint belonged to the stage company, but he ought to get some bonus for almost dying in Butterfield's employ.

"We were held up, but the robbers got chased off."

"You chased them off? Without a guard?"

"The passengers joined in, leastways until one was killed."

As Legrange berated him more for losing not only the cavalry's payroll but a passenger as well, Slocum caught a flash of red from the corner of his eye. He turned and saw a woman with flame red hair retreating into an office. Her face was turned from him, but from what he could see, she was shapely and moved easily, with a liquid stride that made her hips sway just right.

"Slocum!" The captain's bark made the sergeant brace even more stiffly. Slocum merely turned his attention back reluctantly. He had served with CSA officers who thought shouting was the only way to get their men's attention. From his experience with them, they were less effective than a leader who calmly . . . led.

"Seems as if an attempted robbery out on the road is a military matter, payroll or not," Slocum said. "With the entire county destroyed, the sheriff has his hands full."

"I can't leave the fort until my superiors return. I'm in command."

Slocum knew Legrange itched to arrest him, to get out in the field and recover the payroll, to do things a garrison officer never did. For that he approved. Any officer unwilling to get into the field at the head of a column of soldiers wasn't much of a commander. Legrange went up in his estimation. Just a little. If only the officer wasn't so intent on throwing him behind bars.

"Sir," the sergeant said. "I can lead a small detachment."

"We're down to bare bones now, Sergeant Wilson. What do you have in mind?"

"We got three men locked up right now, sir. Nothing serious. Failure to appear for a parade—"

"Folkes was drunk."

"And he's sobered up now, sir, after being locked away

for three days. The other two aren't up on serious charges. Send them out on patrol and erase their charges."

Slocum was getting to like Sergeant Wilson, too. The noncom was looking out for his men. Drunk and failure to report were hardly major charges but might see the soldier drummed out of the Army.

Legrange looked hard at Slocum, then glanced in the direction of the offices where the red-haired woman had gone. From the look of uncertainty replacing his anger, the officer was close to making a decision.

"Do so. I'll sign the orders, Sergeant. Find that damned payroll. And if you have any trail, which I doubt, track down these road agents. But recovering the payroll is paramount."

"Understood, sir." He threw a snappy salute to his commanding officer. Legrange returned it, did an about-face, and marched away.

Slocum waited a moment to follow Sergeant Wilson to see where the captain went. While he walked away from the offices at first, he soon changed direction and went to the office the woman had ducked into.

"That Legrange's office?"

"What?" Sergeant Wilson glanced over his shoulder. "Yeah, it is. He said he'd get my men from the lockup."

"You depend on those three?"

"They're shirkers, that's for certain sure, but they aren't getting paid while they're locked up and they owe me money from last week's poker game."

Slocum laughed at that. Wilson's motives might go beyond simply sticking up for his men. Whatever drove him, he was doing the right thing. Slocum lengthened his stride to keep up with the smaller man's rapid double time pace.

Before they got to the guardhouse, Wilson started shouting to free the three prisoners. By the time Slocum came up behind the sergeant, he had the trio lined up, squinting into the sun because they had been plucked from the jail's dim interior so quickly.

"Listen up, I got the captain to let you out. You're goin' back in and this time you'll get lashes if you so much as look cross-eyed at me."

Slocum turned away as Sergeant Wilson continued upbraiding his men, letting them know they needed to stay on the right side of the bars and that they had to pay him what he had won in the poker game. As Wilson shaped up his soldiers, Slocum saw the red-haired woman standing with Legrange in the doorway leading to his office.

He pulled down the brim of his hat to shield his eyes from the bright Texas sun. The two were standing mighty close together. One could say they were pressing against each other. Then the woman whirled away in a flurry of skirts and rounded the side of the building. In less than a minute, she returned, driving a buggy. Legrange lifted his hand, as if to wave to her, then checked his action. He stared across the parade ground to where Slocum watched, then vanished into his office.

"Get saddled, and do it before sundown, you lazy layabouts!"

"What kinda rations we takin', Sarge? The slop they give us in there's more criminal than anythin' we done."

"Folkes, you ever heard the old saying, 'An army travels on its stomach'?"

"Cain't say I have."

"I'll rip out your belly by reaching down your miserable throat and then put it back by stuffing it up your ass if you don't quit complaining. Stop by the mess hall and grab whatever you can carry with you. Move!" Wilson barked out his command, stood with his balled fists on his hips, and shook his head. "Can't imagine how I ever thought those slackers would ever pay me what I won."

Slocum didn't point out that they weren't likely to pay anytime soon if they didn't find the strongbox carried away by the tornado.

Instead, he said, "I'm not sure my horse can keep up with

your fine cavalry ponies. That old paint is one short gallop away from a glue factory."

"We'll ride slow. Better being out on the trail than in the post." Wilson looked around. "Not a bad assignment, not like Fort Davis, where the outlaws and Indians get away slipping across the Rio Grande. We actually catch some robbers and killers, time to time."

"Before the Rangers?" Slocum saw he had touched a sore point with the sergeant. The Texas Rangers prided themselves on their efficiency at catching crooks and seldom had good things to say for the U.S. Army, save when it suited them.

"Mount up. Folkes and his Gold Dust Twin partners are ready."

The trio rode across the parade ground, stuffing hardtack into their mouths and chasing it down with water from their canteens. Wilson's exaggerated sigh preceded his order for them to refill the canteens before leaving the post. Slocum followed them to a water barrel, drank until he thought he might bloat, then shoved the cork in his own canteen when it was full. This was the first time he had taken to the trail in West Texas with enough water. As he slung the canteen across his saddle and fastened it down, he heard Captain Legrange bellow for Wilson.

The sergeant rode to his commander and silently listened for over a minute. The captain gestured, pointed, then Wilson snapped a salute toward Legrange to signify he understood his orders. Slocum wondered what more the officer had to say to his noncom. He reckoned he would find out in due time.

"You're the scout, Slocum," the sergeant said. "So lead on."

Slocum got his bearings and cut across the prairie in the direction of the main road leading to Gregory. The sun was hot on his left side by the time he reached the road and found the track left by the twister. It had pulled up mesquite by the roots, no mean feat since the taproots could run a hundred yards or more into the ground.

"Yes, sir, that tornado came by," Folkes said. "Lookee there. That looks like part of the stagecoach."

Slocum followed the soldier's gaze and had to agree. He trotted to the spot and saw the door had been ripped from its hinges and spun through the air, not as far as he might have thought but still a quarter mile from the road.

"The strongbox is bolted to a large brass plate. Find high ground and look for any reflection off it," Slocum said.

The three soldiers started to obey until Sergeant Wilson bellowed for them to stop.

"He's not giving you orders. I am." Wilson glowered at Slocum, making him wonder what the captain had said before they left Fort Stockton. The sergeant had been civil enough toward him until Legrange had given his final orders.

"So whatcha want us to do, Sarge?" Folkes curled one leg up and around the saddle horn. Wilson forced him to assume a more military demeanor by glaring hard at him.

"I want you to ride south and look on the far side of the road. Find a hill, look for bright light like Slocum said." He sent the other two in different directions north of the road. When they were out of earshot, Wilson turned and said, "Don't ever try that again."

"You ended up doing what I wanted," Slocum said. Wilson started to give him what for when Folkes fired his pistol in the air.

"What the hell's he doing?" Slocum asked. "Might be he found the road agents that killed my passenger."

"He'd run like hell if he did that. Folkes is not only a lousy poker player, he's got a yellow streak a mile wide up and down his back." Wilson kicked his mount to a gallop. Slocum followed at a slower pace. His ancient gelding wasn't up to such exertion.

"Lookee what I found, Sarge. It's a body!"

Wilson looked down at the body lying facedown on the ground. A huge red spot on the back of the man's coat showed a bullet had gone clean through his body.

"That's my passenger, the one the road agents shot down," Slocum said. He surveyed the countryside and hardly believed this might be the spot where the ambush had happened. More likely, the tornado had picked up the man's body and carried it here, although they weren't far from the main road.

"What's his name?" Wilson asked.

"Don't know exactly. Rafe Stanton said his first name was Fred. Stanton was the only one to get away alive after the twister sent the stage sailing through the air."

"The only one who survived but you," Wilson corrected.

"He ought to have a wallet on him. The outlaws lit out after they killed him."

"Now why'd they do a thing like that?" the sergeant asked. "Piss poor way to rob a stage."

"Might be they saw the tornado coming and hightailed it," Slocum said, but he didn't believe that. The tornado hadn't struck for some time after the passenger had been gunned down. "The road agents were in that direction, firing toward the road."

"They piled up rocks to stop you?"

"No rocks left," Slocum said, looking toward the distant road. He wasn't sure this was the spot where the ambush had occurred. The tornado had rearranged the way the prairie looked. "I moved some of the rocks. The wind might have sent the rest of them sailing."

"Happens," Folkes said. "I seen a rock go clean through three walls in town a couple years back. Twister picked it up in the street and flung it wild like, like it was shot from one of them slingshots you read about in the Bible."

"You don't look like a God-fearing man to me," Wilson said.

"Brung up that way. Drifted from the true path."

"The wind blew the body this far," Slocum said, intent on why they had been sent out from the fort. He dismounted and rolled the passenger's body over. The face was smashed in, and from the way the body oozed rather than flopped, the bones had been pulverized. "No telling how long he spun around in the wind or what he hit along the way before getting spit out here."

"Folkes, go through his pockets. It's nothing you haven't done before," Sergeant Wilson ordered.

"He . . . he looks like a spook. No blood, bones pokin' through his cheeks like that."

Slocum dropped to his knees and pulled back the tattered coat. He fished around until he found the wallet. As he held it up, Wilson snatched it from his hand.

"This is official. I got to verify his identity." Wilson leafed through the greenbacks and looked at Folkes, then Slocum, as if daring them to stop him from stuffing the bills into his pocket. Neither said a word as the sergeant did so, then pulled out a letter and unfolded it.

He scowled and his lips moved as he read. Then he looked up.

"This here letter says our dead man is Fred Sampson."

Folkes jumped as if he had been poked with a needle.

"Why, that's the captain's—"

"Shut up," Wilson snapped.

Slocum stared at the sergeant, waiting to hear an explanation of the man's importance. He didn't get it.

"Sampson's widow's got to be told," was all the noncom said. He tucked the wallet under his broad leather belt and stood, staring at the body. "No doubt he was shot clean through the heart."

"It was either a lucky shot or somebody good with a rifle pulled the trigger," Slocum said. "The road agent had to be a hundred yards away."

"No reason to find the spot where the road agents hid," Wilson said.

The land had been cut up, entire sections shifted around, denuded of vegetation in places and debris piled up in others. The tornado was capricious the way it dipped down to ground and then bounced along, dispensing destruction willy-nilly.

"We ought to bury Mr. Sampson," Wilson said. "Not able to take him back to Gregory or the fort, not when this'd happen 'fore we got a mile." He nudged the dead man's arm. It flopped about, the bones turned to dust.

Folkes turned away and retched. Slocum had seen worse in his day, but nothing quite this peculiar. The tornado had turned Fred Sampson into a meat sack.

"Better get started, but we don't have a shovel. You didn't bring one, did you, Sergeant?"

"Find a piece of the stagecoach and use that to scrape a hole deep enough." He shook his head. "That poor son of a bitch is so mangled up, the coyotes wouldn't even touch him." He shook his head again as he went to find large enough pieces of the stage to use.

It took longer finding more than splinters than it did digging a hole in the prairie. The heavy rain caused by the tornado made digging easier than it might have been until they dug down and found a layer of caliche, but Slocum didn't find it pleasant—or easy—to roll Fred Sampson into the grave. Folkes was almost frantic in his haste to cover the body and hide it from his sight. Slocum stood back and let the soldier work.

"Where'd your other two get off to?" Slocum asked.

"If I know them, they're waiting until we're done, then will put in an appearance. Folkes there would be with them, doing the exact same thing, if I wasn't riding herd on him."

As if on cue when the last of the dirt had been pushed back over the body, the two soldiers rode into view. They whooped and hollered and waved their arms like madmen.

"They found the payroll money!" Folkes cried.

Slocum knew they hadn't. The brass plate would be the

work of the devil to separate from the strongbox. In spite of the tremendous force of the wind, its pulling the bolts out wasn't likely.

Even Sergeant Wilson got excited as the pair of soldiers rode up. His expression faded as he saw they carried two mail bags, not the cavalry's payroll.

"We found 'em a mile over the horizon. Figgered the mail's got to go through."

Slocum looked from the two soldiers proud of their discovery to the grave, then to the sergeant. Without a word, he went to his paint, stepped up, and waited for the command to return to Fort Stockton.

It was a long way back and the noncom's silence was ominous.

4

Captain Legrange glared at the mail bags, as if he could turn them into his post's payroll through pure cussedness. For all Slocum knew, it might work if the officer kept at it long enough.

"Not much else I can do," Slocum said. "I'll report back to Mr. Underwood and—"

"You're not going anywhere, Slocum. You're confined to the post. Sergeant Wilson, see that he stays within the walls."

"Sir!" Sergeant Wilson snapped to attention but cast a sidelong look at his new charge. Slocum wasn't winning any friends at Fort Stockton, and he couldn't understand why they felt that way. He hadn't sent the twister ripping across the countryside and hadn't been responsible for the attempted robbery. If anything, losing only one passenger to the road agents had been a minor victory.

Slocum frowned. Like most of the West Texas forts, there was only a knee-high adobe wall around the perimeter, intended to keep poultry in and small varmints out. It didn't work too well for either chore. Mostly it provided a distinct path for the sentries to walk and gave their superiors an idea where there soldiers ought to be at any given moment of their duty.

"You putting me in a cell?" Slocum didn't make a move toward his Colt Navy. If he had, the inside of a jail cell would be the least of his worries. A dozen troopers marched past on the parade ground. Any threat to their commander would be met with a hail of violence.

"I don't want you running around loose."

"Why not? I haven't done anything but get shot at by road agents."

"The payroll was your responsibility. I'm not sure you didn't hide it, thinking to fetch it later."

"I wouldn't have come out here if that was my intent," Slocum said. "Underwood ordered me out here with the information so you wouldn't be kept in the dark."

"Well, dammit, I *am* in the dark. Where's the gold?"

Nothing would soothe the captain's ruffled feathers. Slocum understood the man's frustration, but he didn't have to put up with it. He wasn't a soldier under Army command.

"Keeping me under your thumb's not going to recover your payroll. Send out more than that sorry ass bunch that escorted me to where the stage was caught up in the twister. You'll have a better chance of paying your soldiers that way." He saw Wilson tense and his hands clench into fists. All Legrange had to do was look the other way and the sergeant would whale the tar out of him.

Or he'd try.

Before any of them could move, the rattle of a carriage distracted both soldiers. Slocum saw the fleeting expression on Legrange's face and turned to find out who the officer was so glad to see. A woman sat next to Underwood, who drove the carriage with some trepidation. The stationmaster obviously was unfamiliar with the rig but did his best to accommodate the woman, who was partially turned and chattering nonstop. Underwood's head bobbed in agreement, but Slocum doubted the stationmaster heard one word in ten from the intent gaze he gave the team. They were friskier than he was used to handling, no matter that he preferred the company stallion to the staid paint he had given Slocum.

"Whoa! Whoa!" Underwood half stood to thrust his foot against the foot board for better leverage tugging on the reins to stop the two horses. He dropped back to the seat and wiped his sweaty forehead.

"Mrs. Sampson," greeted Legrange. He went to the far side of the carriage and took her hand to help her down. She threw her arms around his neck and pulled close, to the captain's obvious surprise.

Surprise, Slocum thought, but not distaste. If anything, he held her a bit too tight, too familiarly. When her bonnet slipped and let out a lock of flame red hair, Slocum wondered if she wasn't the same woman he had seen earlier going into Legrange's office, then driving from the post in a small buggy.

"Slocum!" Underwood climbed to the ground and came over, legs stiff from the drive. "You take soldiers out to find the stagecoach yet?"

"The captain sent me out with four of his men. They found the mail bags but not the strongbox." Slocum looked past the stationmaster to where Legrange still held the red-head in his arms. They reluctantly parted when they became aware of his attention. She dabbed at tears. "Who's that?" Slocum asked.

"The wife of one of the men missing. He was a passenger."

"Does she know?" Slocum frowned. He didn't know how the new widow could have learned her husband was shot down when the soldiers had just reported the fact to the captain.

"She knows her husband didn't make it after the stage was ripped apart by the twister. Only the one what came into town with you survived."

"So you brought her straight out to Fort Stockton?"

Underwood coughed, then looked at Slocum before saying, "Truth is, Miz Sampson insisted on coming out here and made me drive. She was too upset, she said."

"I can imagine," Slocum said. He hadn't gotten a good look at the woman who had been with Legrange earlier, but he would bet his last dime that the grieving widow and Mrs. Sampson were one and the same. How many women with such flame red hair lived in the area?

"You tell her, Slocum," Legrange said, coming over, his arm around the woman's trim waist.

"Tell her what?"

"What you found, dammit." Legrange ground his teeth together, then said, "Pardon my language, Mrs. Sampson. This is greatly infuriating."

"What is it, sir?" She looked at Slocum with wide green eyes. There was no trace she had been crying. Her eyes were bright and clear. "What have you found?" She gripped Legrange's arm and demanded of him, "What did he find, Captain? Tell me!"

"Ma'am, the dead man, the one shot down by the road agents, or so he claims, had this in his possession." Legrange took the wallet from under his belt and held it out.

The redhead took it in steady hands. Then she looked up at Slocum. Her hands shook now and she gasped out, "This is Fred's wallet. My husband. Mr. Sampson."

"There's a letter in there addressed to him, ma'am," piped up Sergeant Wilson. "We didn't read it. Wouldn't have been right reading another man's mail like that, not when we took it off his body 'fore we buried him."

This produced an anguished cry from her. She buried her face in the captain's chest and shook all over. Slocum found himself watching the parts that shook best. That much seemed real.

"Sorry, Mrs. Sampson," Underwood said. His sympathy struck Slocum as insincere as the woman's tears. The stationmaster motioned Slocum over and said in a low voice, "We got mail to deliver, and since you don't have a stage to drive, you're the new rural mailman."

"What's the pay?"

Underwood's eyes widened, then he smiled. "I figgered you right, Slocum. Money's what drives you."

"A man's got to eat," Slocum said.

"Same pay."

The way Underwood said it told Slocum he should have asked for more money. The U.S. Post Office probably paid its couriers more than Butterfield did its drivers. The stationmaster would likely pocket the difference between what the Federals paid for the mail and what Slocum received.

"Give me the horse."

"That old paint's not worth a plugged nickel," Underwood said, pursing his lips. Then he thrust out his hand. "Deal!"

Slocum shook to seal the deal. Riding from ranch to ranch delivering mail was easier than having his teeth chipped from hitting every pothole with the stagecoach.

"Mr. Underwood, could you see Mrs. Sampson back to town?" Captain Legrange tried to put some distance between him and the woman but she edged closer and stropped alongside him like a cat finding a new leg.

"Certainly, Captain. And if you'll give Slocum here the mail bags, he can get to delivering it. The mail's got to go through."

"He—" Legrange bit off his objection. There hadn't been a reason to keep Slocum on the post, and now he found himself forced either to speak out on his earlier decision or let his almost-prisoner go.

"Send out more patrols, Captain," Slocum said. This infuriated Legrange, but Slocum didn't much care.

Private Folkes lugged the mail bags over and dropped them at Slocum's feet. He slung them over his shoulder and went to his paint. *His* horse. The gelding wasn't much, but he hadn't been able to afford a horse of his own before taking the job as stage driver. All he needed was a steady gait to deliver the mail, which shouldn't take more than a few days.

He slung the bags over the paint's rump, mounted, and left without so much as a glance back as he trotted after Underwood and the grieving widow in the carriage. Once outside Fort Stockton's low fence, he matched the carriage's speed and called down to Underwood.

"I need a map showing where the ranches are."

"A good idea. Asking for directions once you're outside Gregory might not help you much. That damned tornado ripped up a lot of homes, and the hailstones damaged even more. The countryside's in turmoil."

Slocum saw how Mrs. Sampson boldly eyed him. Her emerald eyes matched his in intensity. She was a comely woman, not what he would call beautiful but certainly handsome and regular of feature. A sly grin curled her full lips, then broke into a radiant smile when she saw him studying her.

"Sorry about losing your husband the way you did, ma'am," Slocum said.

"He was murdered?" For the first time, her good humor faded and was replaced by something else for just an instant. What that new emotion was, Slocum couldn't tell. It was too fleeting and certainly at odds with how she flirted with him.

"The road agents shot him down. They'd built a rock wall across the road. When I stopped to clear it, they opened fire. We drove them off, but Mr. Sampson caught a round in the chest. He died almost the same instant the slug hit him, so he didn't suffer, if that's any solace for you."

"Oh, yes, Mr. Slocum, it is. Thank you." She bent over and whispered to Underwood. The stationmaster frowned, glared at Slocum, then whispered back to the woman.

Slocum couldn't hear what was being discussed but knew he had to be the center of it from the way the redhead kept looking past Underwood at him. His curiosity about her and Legrange took second place to wondering if he shouldn't just ride away and deliver the mail without returning to Gregory for the map Underwood promised him.

Something kept him riding alongside the carriage all the way into the half-destroyed town. As he approached, again he marveled at the way the twister had danced along one side of the main street, destroying every building above-ground while hardly touching the stores and other businesses on the other side of the street. Capricious, he had heard someone describe a tornado.

"I'll get the map, Slocum," Underwood said. He tied the reins around the brake, got down, and disappeared into the depot.

"Mr. Slocum, I—" She quieted when Underwood came hurrying back, as if he might miss something.

The stationmaster thrust the map into Slocum's hands and said, "Best get on the trail right away. Farms and ranches are marked with small squares. Nothing ought to keep the mail from bein' delivered."

"Ma'am," Slocum said, touching the brim of his hat. To Underwood he said, "I'll get some supplies and be on the trail right away."

He turned his paint's face and started a slow ride toward the far end of town, where the general store still stood. There might not be much left on the store shelves, but he didn't need much to stay alive. More ammunition for his six-gun would go a ways toward letting him hunt for small game out on the prairie, but flour or oatmeal would be appreciated to go with a scrap of meat he had shot.

The store owner apologized for not having any supplies left but was happy when Slocum pulled out a few letters for the man from back East. Somehow, he found a pound of jerky and some canned tomatoes to help Slocum along the trail with his other deliveries.

Slocum was settling the provender behind the mail bags when he heard the soft swish of a woman's skirts behind him. He didn't bother turning to see who it was.

"You want me to check for any mail, Mrs. Sampson?" He finished cinching down his supplies before facing her.

"You are a clever man, Mr. Slocum."

"How's that?"

"You knew who had come up behind you. Are you always so alert?"

"Keeps me alive and kicking."

"I imagine so," she said, giving him a look that would melt iron.

She was bad news, but Slocum felt like a moth fluttering around a flame. She wore her sex like a badge, and Slocum wasn't sure if he didn't want to be arrested. It had been a long, dry spell for him.

"You need something from me?" Slocum asked.

"You *are* perceptive."

"I can mark on a map where your husband's buried, if you want to move him to the town cemetery. Or you might ask Captain Legrange."

"What? What do you mean?"

He saw that this startled her, but she covered her reaction quickly.

"Two of his soldiers were with me to bury the body. He can order one of them to accompany you to the grave site."

"Oh, I see." She came closer and laid a warm hand on his arm. "That's not what worries me the most, John. May I call you John?"

"Reckon you can, Mrs. Sampson."

"Beatrice. I'd like it very much if you'd call me Beatrice."

"What do you want from me, Beatrice?"

"This isn't the place to discuss such a matter," she said. She looked around, her head swiveling from side to side, causing her bright red hair to float away from her pale face in a practiced move meant to draw his attention. It worked. "There. The barn where I park my carriage."

"It's on the wrong side of the street," Slocum said. Her mouth opened, then closed as words escaped her. "I mean that the tornado skipped over it while destroying everything else around it."

"Why, yes, that's so." She took his arm and steered him in the direction of the barn. "You are a complicated man, John. Very deep."

"I like things simple. Not sure what you mean by me being complicated."

"Just tether your horse over there by the water trough. It looks as if it can use some water."

Slocum did as she suggested, then saw she had disappeared into the barn. He looked around, almost expecting to see Captain Legrange waiting for him with drawn pistol. As far as he could tell, he and Beatrice were alone with the horses. He went into the barn's dim interior. Slivers of light slanted through cracks in the walls. One beam caught the woman's hair and turned it into a coppery halo while hiding her face in shadow.

"Come on in, John. What I have to ask is very . . . troubling."

"About you and Captain Legrange?" He saw how she stiffened, then relaxed.

"I didn't know if you'd seen me with the captain earlier. You apparently had. I was at Fort Stockton on business. Serious business concerning my brother."

"Not your husband?"

"Fred was returning from a business trip to Kansas City. I fear his death is wrapped up in my concerns about Joshua."

"Your brother?"

"He . . . this is difficult for me." She moved forward through the bands of warm sunlight, the movement causing her to flicker in and out of shadow like some lovely red-tressed ghost. She stopped before she pressed her ample bosoms against him. She reached up and put her hand on his chest in a calculated move. "He's not quite right in the head. I'm afraid he has gone quite mad."

"How's Joshua and your husband's death connected?"

"That wasn't a robbery attempt. It sounds like something Joshua would do to k-kill Fred. Joshua has become overly protective and thinks I am threatened and wants to keep me safe and—"

Slocum was never sure if he kissed Beatrice or she kissed him. For a moment they hung together, frozen, lips crushing lips. He tried to back away, knowing he was playing with fire. She wouldn't let him. Her arms became steel bands holding him in place and then he stopped trying to fight the inevitable. Her lips tasted like wine and her hair had been freshly washed, smelling of soap with a hint of jasmine.

She broke off the kiss, but he did not retreat because she sank down slowly to her knees. Her hands stroked and caressed and finally grabbed a double handful of his tight ass, pulling him forward. Emerald eyes looked up at him, and a mischievous smile crept over her red lips. Then she began unbuttoning his fly.

His manhood leaped out, stiff and ready. Barely had it been exposed to the air than he gasped. She took him fully into her mouth. Her clever tongue worked up and down the sides, teased the delicate skin beneath the head, and then she pushed forward, taking him down her throat. It was everything Slocum could do to keep from blasting off. It felt as if a keg of Giant powder had been buried in his balls and her mouth was the fuse working down to ignite it.

He laced his hands through her thick, coppery hair and began moving her back and forth in a rhythm that made him even harder in her mouth.

"Umm," she said, pulling back and licking her lips. "You taste wonderful, John."

He pulled her back. She willingly took him into her mouth once more, this time using her teeth a little bit on the sides of his shaft. The flesh tingled and burned and made him even more excited. He closed his eyes and let the wondrous sensations wash through his loins. And when he was sure he couldn't hold back another instant, he felt the saliva on his length turning cold.

She had pulled back and left him hot, hard and needy.

Beatrice fell back onto straw and looked up at him. She slowly raised her knees, then hiked her skirts to reveal her privates.

"I'm not wearing any undies," she said.

Slocum blinked. He could see she spoke the truth now that his blurred vision cleared just a little. Dropping to his knees, he reached out, put his hands on the insides of her creamy white thighs, and pushed them farther apart. She reclined fully and heaved a deep sigh.

"I want you, John. Don't deny me. Don't!"

He pushed her skirts up around her waist so he could move closer. The purpled knob on the end of his shaft banged gently against her nether lips. She shuddered, then lifted her legs, gripping her knees to further expose herself. He slid forward a few inches, barely within her heated center. Both of them gasped at the feelings this caused.

Desire rampaged through him. He thought of the tornado and how it had spun mindlessly, powerful and possessing all in its path. He leaned forward and buried himself another couple inches within her tightness. Then he succumbed. His hips pistoned forward, and he buried himself balls deep within her.

For a long minute, they did not move. Slocum felt sweat beading on his forehead. His arms shook as he supported himself over her. But his hips remained stolid and unmoving. Surrounded by her hot sheath of female flesh, he wanted the desire he felt to last forever. But she twitched, just a little. Her strong inner muscles tensed around him, milking him. He couldn't resist the ages-old urges any longer.

Slocum began stroking, faster, harder, trying to go deeper yet. He rocked her back with every powerful thrust and then the constant motion became ragged. He abandoned himself to pure lust. In the distance he heard her crying out as he felt her clamping down all around him with her orgasm. With a final lunge, he hid himself fully within and then began rotating his hips.

The white-hot tide rose within him and then exploded like a stick of dynamite. He groaned as his hips went berserk. Before he knew it, he was turning limp within her. He looked down into her flushed face. Her eyes were wide, and she could hardly speak.

"I . . . I've never felt anything like that before," she said in a sex-husky whisper. "You're like an animal. And you brought that out in me. Something primitive." Her voice faded.

Slocum got up on his knees and tucked himself back into his jeans. It took him longer than usual to fasten the brass fly buttons, maybe because his hands still shook in reaction or perhaps because he couldn't take his eyes off her.

She wasn't the most beautiful woman he'd ever had but there was something about her that excited him beyond all reason. If she had asked for a second round, he would have been able to do so in only minutes. It might have been the animal in her—in him—or it could have been something more. He wasn't inclined to think hard on it. It was good enough just to enjoy her body and their coupling.

"Joshua," she said softly. "He only wanted to protect me from an abusive husband. Look for him when you're out delivering mail and keep him safe. I don't want the law arresting him. They'd hang him for certain because I'm sure he killed Fred, thinking he was helping me." She scooted back in the straw and pulled down her skirt to chastely hide her privates. "Be careful of him. And never turn your back on him."

"I'm not going to kill him unless I have to."

"I don't want him dead, I want him where he can't hurt anyone else." She leaned back on her elbows and gave him that crooked smile. "When you do, I'll be happy to pay you . . . whatever you want."

There was no mistaking her meaning.

For a grieving widow, she sure did have a way of relieving her heartbreak that appealed to him.

Slocum left Beatrice in the barn, got on his paint, and started out of town to find the first ranch to deliver a package of letters.

5

Slocum had not even reached the edge of town when he heard the dog's loud barking. He drew rein and listened hard. The sound was different than expected from a dog fighting off an enemy, and like wolves, dogs seldom barked when they attacked. They were too focused on killing.

He rode down a side street and let his paint pick its way through the rubble. This was the part of Gregory that had been devastated, though in places some buildings still stood as miracles flaunting a devil wind. The dog raced back and forth, then dropped and put its head on outstretched paws, large brown eyes staring at him. As he approached, the mangy animal jumped to its feet and began barking again.

Slocum swung his leg over his horse and dropped to the ground. The dog went wild in its glee that it had found a human to listen to it. Dropping to one knee, Slocum took the dog's head in both hands and then scratched its ears. The dog tried to pull away, but Slocum wanted to keep it quiet for a moment. The noise the dog had heard so clearly was faint, hardly a scratching sound. It might have been caused by the wind, but the day was preternaturally still after the tornado's full fury.

Releasing the dog, he went to a pile of planks that had once been a building. He took his lead from the dog, who dug and tried to nose away the pile of boards. Slocum lent his aid, and the dog didn't pull away. He kept at his work for ten minutes until he saw a bloody hand poking up through the debris under the pile of lumber. He dug faster when he noticed that blood oozed from the exposed wrist. Dead men don't bleed.

He kicked away a heavy plank and was rewarded with bloodshot eyes staring up at him. The man's lips were swollen from lack of water, and he could only feebly gesture. Slocum understood what he meant, though.

"No need to thank me," Slocum said. "The one you ought to thank is right here." The dog pressed past and began licking the man's bloodied face. While the dog tended his master, Slocum returned to his paint, got the canteen, and brought it back.

He dribbled a few drops onto the man's lips, his tongue, into his mouth.

"Not too much at first," Slocum cautioned. "You need to get used to the idea of water again. You been buried under the rubble since the twister hit?"

The man shook his head. He reached for the canteen. Slocum watched carefully as the man sipped. If he had tried to gulp it all down, Slocum would have taken it away. Over the next fifteen minutes, the man regained his strength and finally sat up, propped by a pile of boards.

"After the tornado," the man grated out. "I had piles of lumber. Thought I could use it in town but it toppled on me. Trapped me for better than a day." He looked around, blinked, and then said, "Might be two days I was caught. Thanks, mister."

"Give your dog a big bone and the debt's repaid," Slocum said. "Let me help you up. Where's the doctor's office?"

"That quack? Vet's office is closer anyway. Trust him. Doc Preston's likely passed out from too much booze."

Slocum put his arm around the man to support him, and they walked slowly away from the center of town. An adobe house—hardly more than a hut—along the road leading west had a small shingle swinging in front. This was the veterinarian's office.

"Anybody home?" Slocum called. The door opened. A man with a bushy beard but hardly taller than a young child opened the door. He pushed his eyeglasses up on his nose and peered at Slocum.

"Another one? Bring him in, but if he says a word, I throw him out."

"His dog saved him," Slocum said.

"Of course the dog did. The animals are the only ones with any sense in this town. Damn shame so many of them got caught in the tornado." The short man hobbled about on legs hardly half the length they should have been.

At first Slocum thought the man might have lost his lower legs in an accident, maybe the war, but tiny feet encased in button shoes put that notion to the lie. The vet was just not as tall as most folks.

"Sit there, Jeb." The vet pointed to a low table. He hobbled over to a cabinet built for his height and rummaged around inside, pulling out bandages and a bottle of carbolic acid. He sloshed some on his hands before beginning his examination.

Slocum stood back and let the veterinarian work. No medical doctor could have patched up Jeb better. In a few minutes his wounds were cleaned and bandaged.

"You're gonna have to stay off that right paw—foot, that is," the vet hastily corrected. "You drove a nail smack through it. Was it a rusty nail?"

"Clean," Jeb said.

"You're likely going to be fine."

"I owe everything to you and this fellow."

"And your dog," the vet said sourly. "From what's been said, you owe him a lot."

"A bone. I promised him a big beef bone."

"Don't renege on that. You do, I find out, I'll charge you double for patching you up. Now get out of here. I got real patients to tend."

Jeb's dog barked and darted about, dashed outside, and led the way. Slocum helped the man into the bright sunlight.

"You got a place to stay?" Slocum asked. "Resting up a spell would help you as much as all the fancy bandaging."

"Not so fancy. Clyde—that's the vet—he knows his job. Takes better care of horses and cows than he does the occasional man going to him."

Slocum helped Jeb back to his tumbledown house.

"I can find bedding in this mess. Shouldn't have stacked so much sawed lumber where the wind could get it. Smashed it into the side of the house, weakened it, and when I got to poking around, it all collapsed." Jeb stood an ottoman upright then sat heavily on it. He thrust out his foot and rubbed his leg. "Be as right as rain in a day or two."

"I've got to be going," Slocum said, "but there's something you might tell me about Gregory."

"If that's all the reward you want, I gotta consider myself lucky. Shoot."

"You know the Sampsons? Fred and Beatrice?"

"Them people at the outskirts of town? Or what used to be the town? Know of 'em, know 'em to see on the street. Always polite but never spoke much with either of them. Specially not the man."

"Why's that?"

"Nasty expression all the time, like he's always mad at something he can't quite spell out."

"What of Mrs. Sampson?"

"You got some interest in her? She's a fine-looking woman, that head of red hair and all. Turns to gold in the setting sun." Jeb coughed. "Not that I noticed such things, mind you. Fred Sampson would never take kindly to anyone looking at his woman."

"He's dead. Killed on his way back to town the day the twister struck."

"Can't say I got any feeling one way or the other. Might be Mrs. Sampson would be happy about it, but don't know. Some married folks, they enjoy the arguing and the makin' up, if you know what I mean."

"What about her brother?"

Jeb's eyebrows arched. He pursed his still swollen lips, winced at the motion, then shook his head.

"Didn't know she had a brother, but then like I said, they weren't the most sociable people around. They only been in town a month or two."

Slocum considered how Beatrice had struck up an acquaintance with the cavalry captain. Or maybe he was seeing more there than existed. If Fred Sampson beat up on his wife, Beatrice might have sought help from the officer.

"Not much in the way of law in Gregory, is there?"

"Nope, not much. You ought to know that coming and going the way you do. You're the stagecoach driver, right?"

Slocum had to admit to being the one.

"I never much took longer in town than I had to. Passed right on through the few months I've been driving for Butterfield."

"Gregory's a doomed town," Jeb said. "Too out of the way for a rail to come through and a lot of roads go to Fort Stockton but not here. Used to be a thriving place, but Fort Stockton gets supplies from all over now, and the railroad's likely to come up from San Antonio, not over to Gregory. Town's doomed, no matter what. And the twister ain't helpin' keep it alive, if you follow my meaning."

"Never even seen anyone with the Sampsons who might be a relative?"

"Can't say I have. You might ask in town. Doc Preston spends more time in the saloon than he does at his office.

He'd know. I'd say you could find him at the Gully Washer but it got all blowed down."

"Wrong side of the street," Slocum agreed. "Only saloon left's on the other side." Gregory had gone from being a two-saloon town to a one-saloon town.

"Wrath of God's more like it, but then the church got turned into toothpicks, too."

"I've got a job to do," Slocum said. "You be all right?"

"Me and the dog'll do just fine, thank you. You ever need a stack of planks for a house or to build a store, they're yours. Might have been under that pile of wood the rest of my life if you hadn't dug me out."

Slocum pointed to the dog so the man would remember the real hero, smiled, then left, finding his paint patiently waiting. Rescuing Jeb had taken the better part of two hours, but information had been gathered that perplexed him more than a little. Whatever had gone on out at the Sampson place was a mystery to most of the townspeople. If he wanted answers—other than those Beatrice would give him—he needed to pry them from Captain Legrange. Why he cared, other than to drive away some of the boredom of not having a real job, was something of a poser.

It might have been the energetic sex with Beatrice Sampson, but Slocum doubted that was the entire answer. Mysteries always drew him like a magnet pulls iron filings, and she was a big mystery. And as much as he hated to admit it, he felt some responsibility for Fred Sampson's death out on the road. He had been in charge of the stagecoach, and a passenger had died. There wasn't a powerful lot he could have done to prevent it, but that was another part of the mystery Beatrice dropped into his lap.

Brother Joshua was a danger rattling around the prairie, shooting up men that needed it. Slocum wondered where Joshua would draw the line since most everyone in West Texas likely deserved his brand of rough justice.

He rode less than ten minutes, heading southward, before

a man sitting beside the road ahead of him waved. Slocum made sure his six-shooter rode easy in its holster, then approached warily since the man wore his bandanna up over his nose, masking his face. From what he could tell, the man wasn't packing iron. There wasn't anywhere nearby to hide a rifle.

"Mister, you help us out? We're in trouble aplenty."

Slocum rode closer and looked around. He didn't see anyone else, but a pair of ruts cut off from the road, went down an incline, then wound about a low hill. An entire company of highwaymen could be hiding not a quarter mile away.

As Slocum brought his paint to a stop, the man stepped forward, pushed his hat back on his forehead, but didn't remove the mask.

"You're that stage driver fella, ain't you?"

"I am."

"Name of, uh, don't tell me, let me think. Slocum! I heard Mr. Underwood talkin' 'bout you. I'm Moses Jeffrey, the telegrapher."

"What brings you out here so far from town?" Slocum asked. He didn't inquire about the bandanna. If the telegraph operator got around to explaining, he would. Slocum remembered seeing him with the stationmaster a couple weeks earlier. The men had argued over something of no real importance, but it had riled both of them considerably.

"All my lines are down. Tornado. Got a couple linemen out workin' to get 'em back up, but there's no tellin' how long they'll be gone."

"So you're like me, a man without a job." Slocum considered asking if Jeffery would be interested in the chore of delivering mail since that wasn't so far from his usual occupation. That would free him of his obligation to Underwood and the stagecoach company, but riding on to find a new town didn't appeal to him as much as it might have hours earlier—before he had taken on Beatrice's errand of stopping her crazy brother from shooting up the whole of West Texas.

"Got one that turns my stomach." Jeffrey put his hand to his mouth, found the cloth, and hastily yanked it down. "Sorry, don't know how that looked to you. I had it to keep from gettin' too sick."

"What's your problem? This is my day for listening to a passel of them."

"I'd be sure to put in a good word with Mr. Underwood if you could help Old George and me. I drove off the road tryin' to avoid a nasty stretch and got mired where it was even worse. Damned rain turned the entire prairie into a swamp and the load's way too much for the wagon."

"You bust an axle? A wheel?"

"Just stuck in a mud pit. Slewed off the road and couldn't right it 'fore we was in trouble."

"You could unload and have the team pull it out that way." The expression on the man's face at the suggestion turned Slocum wary. Jeffrey looked close to puking out his guts.

"I . . . I'd rather not. Old George, he's the town undertaker, and the load we got's gettin' mighty stinky."

Slocum felt a cold knot tighten in his belly. He hadn't seen that many dead bodies in Gregory. Now he knew why. Old George and his new assistant had been hard at work keeping the town from turning into a charnel pit.

"I know you got mail to deliver, but we'd be thankful if you could help." The man's plaintive plea convinced Slocum he could afford to take a bit more time from riding to find the recipients of the letters in the mail bags. They had waited this long. A few minutes longer would not matter to them.

"Come on up," Slocum offered. He grabbed Jeffrey's hand and pulled him behind on the horse. The paint protested the extra load but gamely followed the road down and around the hill to the spot where Jeffrey had driven the wagon off the road.

Slocum saw the problem. The road ran across a

streambed that was usually dry. With the passing storms, the dry arroyo had filled and turned the road into a muddy, slippery morass. The wagon hadn't so much slid off the road as simply bogged down. Jeffrey moved behind him, pulling up his bandanna about the time Slocum caught the stench rising from the wagon bed.

He pulled up his own bandanna and appreciated the smell of sweat and dirt far more than decay.

"You got a sucker to hep us? By damn, man, you got a silver tongue in yer head. I'll give you that free funeral when you need it."

"Old George enjoys his work," Jeffrey said needlessly. Slocum could tell from the undertaker's enthusiasm for his work.

"Would a second horse pulling be good enough?" Jeffrey slid to the ground and sank down midway on his boots in the mud.

Slocum started to answer, but a curious feeling made the hair rise on the back of his neck. He swung around in the saddle and looked at the road he had just traversed. On the ridge above the hill he caught sight of a rider silhouetted by the afternoon sun.

Jeffrey saw his interest.

"Think we can get another hand to help out?"

Before he finished his question, the rider disappeared. Slocum shook himself, realizing he had reached over unconsciously to fill his hand with the ebony handle of his six-gun.

"Don't think we can expect him to stop by," Slocum said.

He rode to where the swayback mule stood in the mud, looking content that it had nothing more to do for the moment. The paint began crow hopping about. The smell of so much death pushed it to edginess.

"You two push, and I'll see to the animals," Slocum said.

When that didn't work, he had to let his horse and the mule pull on their own while he added his shoulder to the rear of the wagon, alongside the undertaker and Jeffrey. Rocking the wagon back and forth broke the suction in the mud, and the animals succeeded in pulling the load of bodies free of the mud. Slocum ran around, grabbed the harness, and kept the mule pulling. His horse veered away and tried to run off. The smell of so much death caused it to snort frantically and its eyes go wide and scared.

"We'll get the load on over to the graveyard," Jeffrey called as he climbed back into the driver's seat. "Much obliged!"

"You got a free funeral comin' yer way, too," Old George said. "Whenever you need it."

Slocum looked back at the empty ridge. That day might come sooner than he'd expected if he wasn't careful out on the trail.

6

Riding with constant vigilance on his back trail began to wear on Slocum. He almost cried out in relief when he came to a ranch house that showed some damage from hailstones but not much else. The barn was in good repair, and the house roof had been recently patched. Nobody was in sight, though, and that worried him.

He glanced back to be sure the phantom on his trail wasn't sneaking close, saw no one, then stood the stirrups and bellowed, "Hello! Anyone here?"

A dog barked. That was his only reply. He sank back into the saddle and rode forward, wary of an ambush. Folks were usually friendly in West Texas, but the storm had turned them against strangers. When he came to the front porch, he waited to see if the lace curtains inside stirred. Not even a breath of wind rustled them. The house was bottled up tight as a drum. He called again.

Again the only reply was the distant dog, and this time it barked hard and loud. Slocum considered leaving the bundle of letters for a Mr. Timothy Yarrow, then decided he needed to hand over the mail personally. A small sign down by the road said this was the Yarrow spread, but anyone could pick up the letters if he only dropped them on the porch. Or they could blow away if there wasn't anyone to take them inside.

He rode around the house, waiting for a rifle barrel to poke out and get him in its sights. By the time he returned to the front, he doubted anyone alive remained inside. But the roof had been fixed within the past few days. The nails poking up from the shingles were still shiny. It would take only a week or two exposure to the West Texas elements to turn them dull.

The distant barking drew him. He rode slowly past the barn, noting that the stalls were empty. One stall needed to be mucked. The piles of horse flop were still fresh, but the horse was nowhere to be seen.

He came to the edge of a cornfield that had been hammered flat by the hail and rain. Able to see across the expanse, Slocum reached for his six-gun. Four men poked at something on the ground. From the sounds, it was the dog. Slocum knew he ought to turn and ride off. Perhaps leaving the mail was the smartest thing. He could tell Underwood he had delivered the packet of letters and be truthful about it.

He put his heels to the horse's flanks and made his way across the destroyed field. When he came within a couple dozen yards, one of the men noticed him. In his hand he held a rope. The lariat circled the dog's neck. Another of the men had similarly roped the dog so they could keep it from attacking by yanking hard on the opposite side. From the frantic, exhausted barks, the dog was close to dying.

"Who're you?" The curt question came from another of them who had been throwing rocks at the dog.

Slocum took in the scene in a quick glance. His Colt slid into his grip easily. He fanned off three shots before any of the men could go for their six-shooters. One shot winged the man who had first spotted him. With a yelp, the man grabbed for his shoulder—and dropped his rope. This was all it took for the dog to launch itself at the other man with the noose around its neck.

Three quick snaps of anger-driven jaws ended that man's life in a bloody explosion from a sundered throat.

Slocum fanned off two more shots. Neither hit pay dirt but the men, seeing their wounded partner and the dead one, let out a yelp and ran. Slocum took careful aim with his remaining round and squeezed off the shot. It flew straight and true, catching one running man in the spine. He threw up his hands and crashed forward, never so much as letting out a squawk. He had died instantly.

Taking the time to reload, Slocum advanced slowly and took a look at the dog, crouched, ears back and snarling. Fresh blood from its kill dripped from its jowls.

"You're on your own," Slocum said, starting to ride away. He stopped when the dog stood upright, ears turning, and let out a bark that was both plaintive and urgent.

Slocum heard the moan that had brought the dog out of its fighting stance. He considered that he might have to shoot the dog if he found its master alive and needing help— and the dog tried to keep him at bay.

Riding in a large circle around the area, he approached a clump of weeds hiding a farmer's feebly twitching body.

"You need help?" Slocum called out. The farmer half rose and reached out to him. He didn't hear any words. Just more moans of pain. "I won't help you if the dog comes for me."

The farmer sank back and muttered until the dog came to him and licked at his face. The man threw his arms around the dog's neck as Slocum dismounted and cautiously approached. He still held his six-gun but wasn't sure if he would actually shoot the dog to help the man. Too many folks didn't deserve it, and except for mad dogs, he had never come across a canine that had double-crossed him.

He slid his pistol into the holster when he saw that the

dog eyed him warily. It drew back its lips in a silent snarl but made no other sign it would attack. Getting his arm under the farmer's shoulders, Slocum lifted him. The man coughed up some blood.

"Damned outlaws. They swooped down and tried to . . . tried to—"

"No need to tell me. They ran off, the ones that could still keep their feet under them. The ones that can't are feed for the buzzards."

"Good." The man spat another bloody gob, coughed up some more, then got better color. "Who're you?"

"Name's Slocum, and I came by to deliver the mail. Your name Yarrow?"

"Yeah," the man said suspiciously.

"Then I have some letters for you." With a heave he got the farmer to his feet. It took a few seconds for the strength to come back to the man's legs. Even then he leaned more on Slocum than walking under his own power.

"You up to riding?"

"Got to," Yarrow said. "Got to get back to the house."

"We'll take it slow."

They rode past the fallen outlaws. Yarrow spat blood in one man's direction but missed the corpse. The simple act of defiance gave the farmer more strength and he made it back to the farmhouse looking stronger than before. He still needed Slocum's help getting down. The whole while the dog trotted some distance away, as if making certain Slocum didn't try anything funny.

"You've got a good dog to protect you the way it did."

"He's a good one," Yarrow said. "Named him Windmill. When he was a pup, he'd lay on his back, all four legs working at the air like he was chasin' rabbits, only goin' nowhere."

Slocum got the man to his porch and into a straight-back chair.

"If you'll be all right, I'll give you the mail and—"

"I can't thank you enough for helping me. They swooped

down like vultures. I spotted 'em coming from up on the roof but couldn't do anything 'bout 'em. They was armed. I ran across the field but they caught me. Me and Windmill."

Slocum heard more in the man's words than he was actually saying.

"You need more help than I've given already?"

"What do you mean?" Yarrow fixed him with a frightened look that told Slocum the story.

"You're not the kind of man to run, not unless there was a reason. Your family? Where'd they hide? You need to go to them?"

"You're really the mailman?"

Slocum snorted and shook his head.

"Not hardly. I was driving the stage to Gregory but got caught up in the twister. It destroyed the stagecoach, but the mail was found. I'm out of a job until the company replaces the stage and team."

"You surely don't have the look of any mail rider I ever did see."

"If Mr. Underwood wasn't paying me, I'd find something else to do." Slocum looked around. "You escaped the worst of the tornado."

"The hail destroyed our crop. Don't call that getting off easy."

"Your house lost a few shingles. Barn's in good condition. What about your livestock?"

"The damned outlaws took my horse and ran off the rest. Had a milk cow and some chickens."

"And a family?"

"I told my wife to take the girls and hole up where they couldn't be found," Yarrow said, coming to a decision about Slocum.

"You tried to lead the owlhoots away."

"Almost worked. House is still standing, even if my livestock's all gone." His eyes darted to the side of the farmhouse.

"Storm cellar?" Slocum asked. "Did they hide there?"

"Nan's too smart for that. Hell, Claudia and Audrey are, too, and they're only nine and seven. No, they lit out for the woods, I reckon. Hard to track in the thicket. Not as bad as in the Hill Country down South, but they could hide just fine in there."

"You up to finding them?"

"I'd be obliged if you could track 'em down and bring 'em back to me." Yarrow spat more blood, making Slocum wonder how badly torn up the man was inside. The outlaws had beaten and kicked him from the look of his overalls and the tears in the heavy denim.

"What should I say so they won't shoot me?"

Yarrow laughed, then choked. He wiped his mouth on his sleeve before looking up.

"You're a savvy fellow, aren't you, Mr. Slocum?"

"My mama didn't raise any fools."

"Nan's a good shot, and she's likely got the rifle. You call out when you find her that we was married in Springfield, Illinois. That's not a thing an outlaw would know."

Slocum considered this a thin thread to hang his life on since the woman knew the wooded area around the farm better than he ever could. She would be holed up where she had a good shot at anyone coming after her and her children. If her husband showed his face, all was well. Anyone else was likely to get a slug in his guts.

"Think Windmill'd come along with me?"

Yarrow considered it a moment, then nodded.

"He's taken a fancy to you. Might come from saving him."

"Come on, Windmill," Slocum said. The dog yelped and then trotted ahead of him in the direction taken by Mrs. Yarrow and her two girls.

Slocum kept a sharp eye out for trouble ahead. The woods and the undergrowth were as he suspected. She might be in a tree or lying on the ground. Either afforded her some protection and the chance to get off more than one round.

Barely had he entered the dim thicket than he heard a childish giggle. He stopped dead in his tracks.

"Windmill, go find 'em," he told the dog. Windmill yelped, then raced deeper into the woods in the direction where Slocum had heard the barely suppressed laughter. The children were playing a game and hadn't seen him approaching. He doubted the woman was as lax.

"Hello, Mrs. Yarrow, my name's John Slocum. Your husband's needing you back at the farmhouse. He said to let you know you were married in Springfield and that would tell you I don't mean you and the girls any harm."

He heard a rustle in the bushes but turned away from them. The woman had tied a thread around some limbs and tugged on it to distract the unwary. She would have had a good shot at his back if he had fallen for the trick. As it was, he faced her as she sighted along the rifle barrel. There wasn't so much as a quiver as she pulled it snug to her shoulder.

"He needs you."

"Who are you?"

Slocum explained about delivering the mail, went through much the same explanation he already had with her husband, and then was rewarded by her lowering the rifle from her shoulder.

"I don't trust you."

"Would it make you feel any better if I handed over my six-shooter?"

"You'd do that?"

Slocum nodded.

"Never mind. We'll go see Simon."

Slocum hesitated, then said, "That what you call your husband? The name on the letters was Timothy."

Now she lowered the rifle all the way and slumped. For a moment, Slocum thought she was going to faint, but she caught herself, heaved a deep sigh, and then stepped from the blind where she had hidden.

"You want your children to stay out here until you're sure it's safe, I won't object," he said.

The two girls came up with Windmill. The dog dashed around them, then came to Slocum and sat, staring up at him. Then the dog barked, got to its feet, and hurried to the girls.

"That dog's got fleas," Mrs. Yarrow said. "He's also a better judge of character than Timothy ever was."

"Good to know that he has fleas," Slocum said, smiling. This brought a broad grin to her face.

Together they returned to the house. When she saw her husband, she shoved the rifle into Slocum's hands and ran to him, knelt, and began wiping away the blood.

"I don't think he's punctured a lung," Slocum said, "but he's likely got a busted rib. That'll heal if you tend it."

"He saved me. Me and Windmill," Yarrow said. "The outlaws stove me in good, then were abusing the dog."

"That explains the blood all over him," she said. Her eyes went wide when Yarrow and Slocum exchanged a long glance. The woman put her hand to her mouth. "I owe the dog more 'n I thought," she said in a small voice.

Slocum knew her husband would get around to telling her the entire story eventually. At the moment, it was more important to get him patched up, just as he had fixed his roof. Any damage that went unfixed always got worse.

"I'll help you get him inside." Slocum got his arm around Yarrow's shoulders and helped the man to stand. He swung him around and started for the open door when the first round ripped past and sent splinters flying in all directions. The next took Slocum off his feet, to land flat on his back. Pain filled his chest and the world swam about in crazy circles.

All he knew was the pain and new bullets sailing through the air.

7

Slocum twitched. His legs kicked and the shiver ran the entire length of his body. He heard distant gunfire, then slowly realized it wasn't that distant. Slugs tore through the air above him as he lay flat on his back.

"Get him inside, Timothy!"

The voice rang in his ears. It took Slocum long seconds to recognize it as the woman he had found out in the woods. A loud moan of pain sounded as hands grabbed his ankles and began dragging him along. He tried to fight but was weaker than a kitten. The moans grew louder and the hands left his feet, only to be replaced by other, stronger ones. He sailed along the rough wood floor until he looked up into Mrs. Yarrow's strained face.

"You pulled me inside?" His voice grated in his throat.

"Timothy's not able. Got busted ribs, like you said. I can feel them. And he surely can, too." She looked at her husband with a mixture of pity and love.

He forced himself up on one elbow and saw that the man had gone pale under his tan and the mask of dirt on his face. When he coughed, he spat up more than a gob of blood dotted with pink froth. Slocum doubted the man had long to live if his lungs were filling with blood.

"Who's shooting at us?" He shook his head and got the beehive of buzzing insects to go away. Coming to his feet, he steadied himself against the wall as he looked out. A slug nearly took his life. Slocum ducked back out of sight.

"Must be them outlaws," Timothy Yarrow grated out from between teeth clenched against the pain. "All we got's the rifle the missus has. Never had no call for a side arm."

"It was a luxury we could not afford," the woman said bitterly, now obviously regretting spending the few dollars on something else.

Slocum glanced around the sparsely furnished house and thought they had probably used the price of a pistol for seed grain or something similar. None of the money had been squandered on fancy furniture or knickknacks to feed the woman's vanity. If anything, the Yarrow family was barely squeaking by.

"If it's the outlaws I ran off," Slocum said, "there are only two of them and one's wounded."

"There's nothing here they could possibly want. They ran off our livestock." Yarrow tried to stifle a cough and ended up spitting blood through his fingers.

Slocum wondered if they might want the mail he carried, then realized he was still blurry from the fall he had taken. The outlaws had been torturing the dog before he had arrived.

"You know them? This might be something personal?"

"Never laid eyes on them before," Yarrow said. To his wife, "Get the girls. Back to the woods. You, too, Slocum. I can hold 'em off long enough for you to get away."

"No!" Mrs. Yarrow's denial came fast and hard. "I'm not leaving you."

"I'll take them on and give you a chance to get to the woods," Slocum said. "You know it and can hide where no man can find you."

"No."

Slocum looked at her, then glanced toward the two girls. They had their arms around the dog's neck.

"Girls, you take Windmill and go to your special place in the woods," their mother said. "Your pa and me and Mr. Slocum have to tend to those terrible men."

"We want to stay."

"Audrey, do as I tell you."

It took a few minutes of family argument. Tears flowed. Slocum ignored what was being said and took the chance to scout where the outlaws were. One was behind the water trough. The other he couldn't locate. That worried him. He might be able to eliminate the one he knew about, but didn't want to catch a bullet because he'd put himself into a crossfire.

"I'll flush out the second man," Mrs. Yarrow said. She shoved the rifle past Slocum's ear and fired, almost deafening him.

He saw that she had chosen her spot well. Her slug ripped through a clump of prickly pear cactus and caused the missing outlaw to yelp.

Slocum didn't waste any time while the outlaw was concerned with being shot at by the woman. He ducked low, slid out the front door, and dodged the best he could to get to the side of the house. From this vantage he had a good shot at the one behind the trough. He got off three quick shots, winging the man. Slocum cursed under his breath. He had hoped to end the man's miserable life then and there. Now he had to deal with return fire and was exposed.

He dived, hit the ground, and skidded along until he came to a halt behind a woodpile. The man behind the trough was wounded. He was the one who'd been shot earlier and had a fresh hole in his shoulder from Slocum's most recent fire. He smiled without humor when he saw the man had to swap hands with his six-shooter. His right arm hung limp and useless.

Taking a chance, Slocum ran from the woodpile using

another round as cover and almost died. The man could shoot as good with his left hand as he did with his right. Having committed himself and not seeing anywhere he could take shelter, Slocum ran on, knowing he had only two rounds left now. The frontal assault caused the man to pause for an instant, and this was all Slocum needed. Two more rounds ended another life.

And then he faced the man's remaining partner, his Colt Navy empty.

He ran as hard as he could with the notion of grappling with the man. He saw the outlaw take careful aim and fire. The slug slammed hard into Slocum and stopped him in his tracks. He tried to reach out and felt himself falling. As he smashed into the ground, all he knew was pain in his gut. Then Slocum blacked out.

How long he was unconscious was something of a poser. It seemed as if he had been out of the fight for only a few seconds, but the sunlight slanting into his eyes told him it was late afternoon, almost sundown. Forcing himself to hands and knees, he tried to shake off the grogginess. He flopped over and sat in the dirt. He touched his belt. The outlaw's bullet had cut through his gun belt as it slammed into his belly. This was what had brought him down. But other than the new hole in his belt and a nasty bruise behind it, Slocum was untouched.

It finally occurred to him to worry about the remaining outlaw. He spun around in the dust and saw the outlaw he had shot facedown on the ground behind the water trough. Fumbling at first, then with more sureness to his touch, he reloaded and went exploring to find what had happened while he was unconscious.

There was no sign of the one who had shot him. The silence shrouding the farmhouse made him fear the worst. A quick check of the house confirmed his suspicions. Nan Yarrow lay sprawled on the porch, still clutching the rifle. From a quick look, he saw that she had been shot at least four times. The bullet through the side of her head had killed her outright, if the others hadn't.

Pushing inside, propping himself against the doorjamb, he saw Timothy Yarrow seated in a chair. The man had likely died before his wife. She might have seen this and stepped onto the porch to take her revenge.

But what of the children?

Slocum called but got no reply. He prowled about and found no sign of them or their dog. The lowlifes had been torturing the dog. If they had taken the little girls, he feared what they might do. It would be better if the two girls had died with their parents.

Try as he might, Slocum couldn't find any tracks left by the girls or the outlaw. It was getting too dark for real tracking. Slocum gave up his hunt for spoor and set to the task of digging two graves. He put the Yarrows side by side some distance from the house on a small rise. Then he got his paint, made sure the mail bags were secured, and started riding through the dark in the direction of Fort Stockton.

He arrived at the fort just before dawn, bone tired and wobbling in the saddle.

"Halt, identify yourself!" came the challenge from the alert sentry.

Slocum did so and asked to be taken to Captain Legrange.

"Captain might not want to talk to you. He's got a powerful lot of worry right now," the sentry said, nervously running his hand up and down the barrel of his carbine.

"That'll be enough, Private," snapped Sergeant Wilson, marching up. "Didn't expect to see you again, Slocum. You get lost?"

"Something like that. Have a road agent that needs taking care of."

"So you hightailed it straight here to the U.S. Army? That's real clever of you," Wilson said. "Get down. Let's talk." He dismissed the sentry.

Slocum stepped down wearily. He hadn't realized how much his entire body hurt. Every bone ached and every muscle felt as if he had dipped it into liquid fire.

"Where'd you run afoul of this varmint?"

Slocum quickly filled the man in. He watched the sergeant's face go through a rainbow of emotions. The usually cynical noncom sucked in a deep breath, then let it out slowly.

"You think the outlaw stole away the little girls?"

"Couldn't find any trace of them," Slocum said. "I can only think of one reason a man like that would take young girls."

"I can think of a couple more, and they're no prettier. There's a big trade with Mexico for *putas*, the younger the better."

"They can't have too much of a head start. It took me six hours to ride here. Get in the saddle right away and we'd overtake them in a day or two, especially if the girls slow the man down."

"The captain's dealing with a powerful lot of woe right at the moment," Wilson said. "He just got word that Major Conrad was caught in the twister, him and his entire company. Not more 'n five survived, and the major wasn't one of the lucky bastards."

Slocum said nothing to this. He caught an undercurrent in what the sergeant said linking the two officers closer than most.

Wilson saw he understood.

"They went to West Point together, were best friends for years. The cap's takin' it mighty hard." Wilson spat. "Moreover, there ain't a dozen troopers that could be spared, and I don't know he'd send any of them out when there's other trouble brewin'."

"I didn't know the Yarrows, 'cept the time I told you about, but I can't let those girls be sold across the river. Can you spare some victuals?"

"You'd give up deliverin' mail for Underwood to track them down? This something personal with you, Slocum?"

"Just doing my duty as I see it."

"How's that?"

"With Timothy Yarrow and his wife dead, that means I have to deliver the mail to the next of kin. That's those two girls."

Sergeant Wilson stared at him a moment, then burst out laughing.

"You are one hell of a barracks lawyer, Slocum. You wait here. I won't be more 'n a few minutes."

Slocum shifted from foot to foot, mentally replaying everything he had seen that might give him a lead on going after the outlaws. The best he could think, considering he hadn't seen hoofprints, was that they had gone west. That made sense since it was only a week's travel to get across the Rio Grande. If they wanted to sell the girls, that was the shortest route to a few pesos jingling in their pockets.

He looked up to see Wilson astride his horse with a large package in his arms. The sergeant tossed it to Slocum.

"That's enough for both of us, 'less you're a big eater."

"Both?"

"The captain won't miss me for a day or two, not with his grievin'."

"Like hell," Slocum said. "You're going AWOL?"

"Can't say that's the way I see it. Besides, you can defend me at a court-martial, if it comes to that. There're only two outcomes. I get killed, in which case it doesn't matter so much what the captain does to me. Or I find the girls and bring them back. He might be mad, but he'd be more inclined to give me a medal than drum me out or stand me in front of a firing squad."

"There's a third possibility," Slocum said, snugging down the supplies and mounting. He looked hard at the sergeant. "We might not find the outlaw or the girls."

Wilson shook his head.

"That's not going to happen." He rode to the sentry, leaned over, and spoke rapidly for several minutes. The guard obviously argued, then was quieted. Wilson rejoined him. "Folkes is going to be mighty surprised to find he has temporary corporal's stripes while I'm gone."

He rode off so fast that Slocum had to push his horse a mite more than he liked to catch up.

"Why're you doing this?" he asked.

Wilson took a deep breath and stared ahead. The sun has risen enough to warm Slocum's back and cause sweat to bead on his forehead, but the moisture he saw on the cavalry sergeant's cheeks wasn't sweat.

"Me and the missus, we lost two girls to the flu a year back. Hasn't been the same 'tween us." He looked at Slocum, face as hard as stone. "She can't have no more children and those two were the sun and the moon to us."

Wilson said no more as he urged his horse to an even quicker gait. This time Slocum let him ride on ahead since his paint was tuckered out from riding for hours already. Besides, he knew when a man needed to be alone. He wasn't averse to simply riding and not jawing either.

When they arrived at the Yarrow house, it was late afternoon. Wilson let his horse drink from the trough where the dead outlaw had stunk up the place. Slocum hadn't bothered burying him. It didn't seem fitting to go to the effort, not when he had put the man and his wife into graves away from the house.

"I recognize this yahoo," Wilson said. "He's one o' the five Terwilliger boys. Their pa got a ranch twenty miles from here."

"Tight family?"

"Couldn't be tighter," Wilson said. "When you killed one of them, Bert here and the others couldn't let it be. They had to even the score. Blood demanded it."

Slocum's mind raced. A family so close hadn't come back to bury one of them cut down in a gunfight. That told him they had better things to do—and that might have to do with kidnapping two little girls.

He took out his six-gun, checked the cylinder, then nodded to the sergeant.

"Let's ride. We've got business to attend to."

8

Slocum couldn't find tracks anywhere he looked. The recent twister and the hailstorm around it counted for some of the problems he experienced, but he had to admit he was unusually anxious, and this robbed his keen eyes of their usual skill. He stood in the stirrups and looked across the increasingly sparse ground. The prairie was turning into desert. If they traveled another couple days, they would get through Wild Rose Pass to Fort Davis in the mountains and not far beyond that roared the Rio Grande. Cross it and Mexico opened up wide and inviting to any road agent.

Or kidnapper.

He seethed at the thought of how he had let one Terwilliger boy get away from him. He felt some obligation to the Yarrow girls because he had not kept the outlaws from killing their pa and ma. It wasn't his job, but he had been there and had failed. That galled him. He had seen too many orphans during the war to ever get used to the notion. The reason William Quantrill had told Bill Anderson to kill him was how he had protested the Lawrence, Kansas, massacre. Quantrill had ordered every male over the age of eight cut down without mercy—and Slocum had seen some of the Raiders mowing down children even younger. And not worrying about their gender.

The tornado had ravaged the land, taken lives, and destroyed towns, but it was not likely to come back and follow the same track. Outlaws like the Terwilliger brothers never stopped returning like bad pennies until they were stopped. Two lay dead with his bullets in them. One had had his throat torn out by a dog. One more would be buzzard bait before he stopped.

"Don't see anything," Wilson said. The sergeant took a long draft from his canteen, then stuffed the cork back in and looked longingly at it, obviously wanting more. He was an experienced trooper and knew finding water out here in the arid land was increasingly difficult.

"You say their spread is close?"

"Think so," Wilson said. "I've ridden on patrol this way a time or two. The captain would be a better one to answer that. Before the twister struck, this was his patrol area. Fort Concho patrols to the north and Fort Davis comes in from due west."

"Don't see any cattle or much of anything to show this land is claimed."

"The Terwilliger clan's never been much for decent work. We keep an eye on them, but they range wide enough to give us headaches following them."

"Not this time," Slocum said. "This time they can ride to the gates of hell, and I'll be on their heels."

"You ever been a lawman, Slocum? No, didn't think so. But you've got the fire in your belly to track these miscreants." Wilson spat, then rubbed his chapped lips. "You might be better suited as a Texas Ranger."

Slocum snorted in disgust. He and the law seldom saw eye to eye. More times than he cared to think on, he had been on the robbing side of the six-shooter when he stopped stagecoaches and entered banks. The lawless behavior wasn't anything to be proud of, but sometimes the crook was more honest than those being robbed. Other times, it had been all Slocum could do to keep body and soul together.

He was not an entirely honest man, but he had never kidnapped small girls after murdering their parents.

"When we follow that road yonder, we'll go straight to them," Wilson said, pointing. He shielded his eyes against the sun, then added, "Looks like they're coming to us."

Slocum squinted and caught sight of a pair of riders traveling north. His heart beat a little faster. The two were alone.

"It's never easy, Slocum. Never," Wilson said, answering Slocum's unspoken complaint. "We can ride parallel to them. That road curves around and will come our way. We can wait for them to come to us."

"Where are they riding?"

"Could be to Fort Concho. They're rumored to supply white lightning to post sutlers, though they aren't carryin' anything this time. Could be they're headin' elsewhere."

"Let's talk it over as we ride," Slocum said. "I don't want to let them get too far away if they don't follow that road into our guns."

"Yes, sir, Slocum, you're not a man I'd want on my trail. You get a thought lodged in your head and nothing shakes it loose."

They rode in silence until Slocum saw a decent spot for an ambush. The flat countryside didn't provide much cover but the road went down into a ravine, with dirt embankments on either side. Get a rider below and they could get the drop on him.

"I'll take the far side. You have a rifle?"

Slocum shook his head. He had been lucky enough to get the horse from Underwood. He reached back and made sure the mail bags still rode over his saddlebags. The supplies Wilson had taken from Fort Stockton's mess hall were half gone now, but Slocum didn't bother getting rid of any extra weight. The paint walked along stolidly, but should he have to give chase, the horse wasn't up for a long gallop, or even a shorter one. The old horse was steady, not frisky.

With luck, there wouldn't be any need for pursuit.

"I'll get as far down the hillside as I can," Slocum said, drawing his Colt and brandishing it. "Your carbine's the only long gun we have to do the job."

"And a carbine's not much for long-range shooting. It'll be better than a handgun, though." Wilson touched the pistol holstered butt-forward at his right hip.

They didn't have much firepower. They had to depend on surprise.

"We need to find where they took the children," Slocum said. "Might be good we don't have better weapons."

"It's never better," Wilson said sourly. "Always better to outgun your enemy, even if you don't have to use it." He put his heels to his horse and galloped down the incline and across the road. His horse struggled up the embankment, then the sergeant disappeared from sight.

Slocum had to rely on the noncom's expertise. From all he had seen and heard from Wilson, there wouldn't be any trouble on the far side of the draw. He found a spot to tether his horse, then worked down the hillside to a point where his six-gun would be useful in stopping the Terwilligers as they rode past.

He expected to have a wait. The two riders trotting through the draw so soon surprised him. Slocum drew his six-shooter and cocked it, taking a bead on the lead rider.

"Stop! Reach for the sky!"

He didn't know where Wilson was, and it might be possible the sergeant hadn't gotten into position yet, but Slocum saw no way he could wait. The two men looked around frantically. One went for his six-gun; the other obeyed.

Slocum shot the man going for his pistol. The Terwilliger slumped forward, and Slocum made a mistake of trying to get a second round into the man. He missed, giving the other brother the chance to drag out his own hogleg. The air filled with white smoke as the three of them began firing. Slocum emptied his Colt, stopped to reload, and found himself scrambling for cover as lead tore through the air all around him. Worse, he couldn't see which of the men was firing at him because the draw held the gunsmoke as surely as any chimney.

When he heard the sergeant's carbine bark, he knew the fight was theirs to lose. Hastily reloading, he kicked out and slid down the hill past the worst of the smoke and crashed into a rock near the bottom. Horses' hooves kicked up a fuss. Slocum had no compunction about shooting at the Terwilligers' mounts. One slug nicked a forelock, causing the horse to rear and throw its rider. Slocum took aim and squeezed off a shot, only to hear the hammer strike a dud. He quickly cocked the six-gun again but the fallen Terwilliger rolled away. His horse pawed the air and prevented Slocum from getting a good shot. He squeezed off another round. Another dud.

Cursing, he wondered if he was doomed to die because all the cartridges he had loaded were duds. The ebony-handled pistol bucked reassuringly in his hand as he fired a third time, but the slug only added to the confusion, not the destruction.

And then there was only silence.

"Wilson, you hit either of them?"

"Not sure. You?"

"Winged one. Shot his horse, too." Slocum dropped onto the road and went into a crouch, looking around to be sure he wasn't on the receiving end of the death he had tried to mete out.

Duck walking to the fallen outlaw, he cursed his bad luck. Before he had wanted to kill the man. Then he hoped to take a prisoner to find out where the girls were. Now he saw he had achieved his first goal. There was a bloody wound in the man's shoulder—the first time he had found a target. Whether it was another of his shots or one Wilson had taken to end the outlaw's life with a bullet that had gone clean through his head didn't matter. He wasn't interested in counting coup or putting notches on his six-gun handle.

"One's dead. You got the other one?" Slocum called to the sergeant. He heard rocks cascading downhill, and in a few seconds Wilson stood beside him, clutching his short-barreled carbine.

"Don't know where he got off to," Wilson said. He knelt, plucked the pistol from the dead man's hand, and jammed it into his broad leather belt. "You might find his horse and see if he's got a rifle you can take. He's not gonna use it anymore."

"I want the other brother," Slocum said. He prowled the narrow draw and found the tracks coming in. Then he saw a single set of hoofprints leading back. They hadn't killed the other outlaw but had spooked him into running.

"Here's his horse. You shot him in the leg. Don't think there's anything we can do for him, 'cept one thing," Wilson said, leading the hobbling horse by the reins.

Slocum spun, aimed, and squeezed off a round. Another dud. He triggered another round. This one took both Wilson and the horse by surprise. The horse reared, then collapsed, the bullet lodged in its brain.

"I thought I heard a couple duds in the fight. You need better ammo."

"Might have gotten wet," Slocum said. "I've got what I've got."

"Here's Terwilliger's rifle. I think that one's Eddie Joe. That likely means Leonard is left. Leonard and his pa. Pa Terwilliger's been laid up with gout for years. Makes him meaner than a stepped-on rattler, but he doesn't stray far from their ranch house."

"Back that way?" Slocum shielded his eyes and tried to spot the rider. He didn't even see a dust cloud.

"If we ride like we mean it, we can get there about the same time Leonard does."

Slocum looked at the dead horse. It would have been a sturdier ride than his paint, but he had to make do with the old horse, just as he had to depend on the punk ammunition. Either might fail him at a vital instant, but he had no choice but to press on. He gripped Terwilliger's rifle, then began making his way up the hillside, slipping in the loose dirt and rocks but eventually reaching the spot where his paint waited nervously. It hadn't taken kindly to all the gunfire.

He gentled the horse, fished around in the supply pack, and found a couple sugar cubes to give it, then waited for Wilson to join him. The soldier made it from across the road and uphill faster than Slocum would have thought.

"We head back along the ridge, cut down to the road and across country. Leonard's likely to follow the road back to his place. Ain't got the sense God gave a goose, that one, but it doesn't make him any less dangerous. If anything," said Wilson, "it might make him more inclined to kill first since he's sure everyone's laughing at him."

"I won't laugh at him," Slocum promised.

The paint protested him mounting, but then valiantly pressed on, keeping the quick pace set by Sergeant Wilson. They crossed the road and trotted over the prairie toward a ramshackle house just as the sun was setting.

"Not sure it's to our advantage trying to take them in the dark," Wilson said. "Leonard's not too bright, but his pa is. There might be all kinds of traps set to stop anyone from sneaking up on the house."

Slocum dismounted, knocked out the rounds in his pistol, then reloaded, checking each round the best he could in the golden rays of the dying sun. He might have a misfire or two, but he had done what he could to make sure each round was good. Only then did he pull the rifle out and examine it.

"Rusty."

"Goes with what I knew of Eddie Joe. Lazy son of a bitch. You be careful that rifle doesn't blow up in your face, Slocum."

"I'll scout the place."

"Hell, that's a waste of time. We both go in together. Why find they're home, then come back for me?"

Slocum had never intended to return to report to the sergeant. If he found Pa and Leonard Terwilliger, he would cut them both down after he found what had happened to the girls. If it took a while to convince the two outlaws to tell him, he didn't want the voice of law and order telling him he couldn't use tricks he had learned from the Apaches to get that information.

"We need them alive," Wilson said softly. He checked his carbine, then the pistol thrust into his belt. He made no effort to check the loads in his service pistol.

Slocum bent low and began moving toward the dark house. Before he had gone a dozen paces, a light flickered in a window, then steadied. Someone had lighted a coal oil lamp. On the heels of the light came angry shouts. Slocum froze and listened hard.

"Dead? Yer brother's dead?"

"Pa, all four of 'em are. Same fella. We tried to get him at the farmhouse. Kilt a woman there and her man was already dead, but this fella . . ." Leonard Terwilliger's voice trailed off.

"You are the stupidest son of a bitch I ever did see. I knowed I shoulda put you in a burlap bag and drowned you along with that litter of kittens the day you was birthed."

"Pa, he might be comin'. Eddie Joe didn't kill him 'fore he got his head blowed clean off."

"And you made a beeline back, bringin' him in like the plague. You ain't got sense enough to—"

Pa Terwilliger bit off his denunciation of his only surviving son when Wilson let out a screech of pure pain.

"Slocum," the sergeant gasped out, "stepped on a bear trap. Told you they'd planned to hold off an army. Get 'em, but be careful."

"Your leg?"

"Might be broke. I'll do what I can from here."

Slocum was torn between returning through the dark to pry open the iron jaws of a trap to free the soldier and pushing on. Any hope of surprise had disappeared with a single incautious footstep.

The light was snuffed out and the metallic click of a rifle being cocked sounded in the still evening air. Slocum felt all prickly, sure the men were sighting in on him. He dropped to his knees, then fell flat on his belly with the rifle snugged into his shoulder.

He fired at the first sign of movement. A crash sounded, quickly followed by Pa Terwilliger's angry words.

"You cain't up and git yerself kilt, Leonard. I won't let you die on me!"

Slocum had a good sense of when he hit a target and when he missed. His single shot had felt solid. He cursed under his breath since he wanted the men alive. Killing Leonard had a benefit, though, and he expected it to come about in a hurry. If Pa Terwilliger was laid up with gout as Wilson claimed, he was likely to use the girls as a shield to get away.

Sounds like a man with a wooden leg came from the front of the house. For an instant Slocum saw a darker shadow crossing a lighter one. Instinct took over. He fired again.

"Damnation, Slocum, you're too good a shot," Wilson said, crawling up beside him. He dragged his leg behind through the dust.

"I didn't think they'd die that easy."

"Let's go see if they're playin' possum or you did nail the sons of bitches." Wilson grunted as he used his left hand to pull his leg up and get it under him. The carbine served as a crutch as he got to his feet. "Don't think any bones are broke, but it hurts like hellfire."

Slocum scrambled to his feet and advanced, as wary of the ground as he was the chance one of the Terwilligers was still alive and would take a shot at him. He found three more hidden traps, pointed them out to Wilson as he trailed behind, then reached the front porch.

A man so fat he drooped off the sides of the wide wooden plank porch lay still. Slocum poked him a couple times and got no response. He shoved the rifle muzzle hard into the man's belly. The flab didn't even twitch.

"This one's dead. Must be the old man."

"Is," Wilson confirmed. "You be careful going into the house. I heard tell they booby-trapped it like they did their yard."

Slocum kicked in the door and was glad he didn't immediately follow. A heavy beam with railroad spikes pounded through it fell straight down and would have skewered him. He stepped over it, pressed his back against a rickety wall, and slowly worked around to the still dark form on the floor. Slocum had been a sniper during the war and had never made a shot as accurate at this one. His round had gone into Leonard's left eye and killed him instantly.

"The one time I wanted to miss . . ."

"Dead, too?" Wilson used his rifle to poke at the deadfall that had missed Slocum.

"Too damned dead for my liking."

"You know what that means?"

"We start searching for the girls," Slocum said.

They didn't find them.

9

"Your aim's too good, Slocum," Sergeant Wilson said. "It would have been a damn sight easier if one of them had been left alive to tell us where they hid the two girls."

"I can say the same about your shooting."

The men stared at one another, then squared their shoulders. Wherever the Terwilliger boys had put their kidnap victims, it wasn't inside the house.

"My leg's all cut up. You'll have to take the barn and the outbuildings. I'll poke around here looking for the girls where I can," Wilson said. "Might be the Terwilligers didn't want to let them get too far out of sight but hid 'em real good." He stomped on the floorboards and broke through. He hobbled around, pulled over a three-legged stool, and sat on it, fingers prying back the boards. "Nope, no sign of a root cellar."

"There must be a storm cellar somewhere," Slocum said. He left the sergeant to his task of ransacking the house. No matter what they found, it wasn't going to be anywhere near as important as the two Yarrow girls.

Slocum made a quick circuit of the ill-kept yard and went

to the barn. The horses would be useful and weren't going to do the Terwilligers any good, but he wasn't interested in horseflesh as much as he was in listening for small voices crying for help. Try as he might, he couldn't hear what he wanted to most of all.

A careful search of the barn revealed nothing. There wasn't the smallest trace that anyone but the family had been here. Prowling farther afield, he found an old shed stuffed full of useless, broken tools and furniture that had outlived any usefulness years back. When he found the storm cellar, his heart beat a little faster. There was a sturdy plank that had been run through the iron handles on the double doors— perfect for keeping somebody imprisoned.

He kicked away the plank and threw open both doors. The darkness below was impenetrable. He called, "Audrey? Claudia? You in there? It's me, Slocum."

No answer, not even a whimper. He fumbled in his pocket and found the tin of lucifers, dragged out one, and scraped it along the bit of sandpaper he had stuck to the back of the waterproof container. The match flared and put out a thick sulfur smell. He held the light at arm's length, then carefully went down the ladder into the storm cellar. Once his foot touched the dirt floor, he slowly turned from side to side, casting the flickering light all about. The Terwilligers had put up some preserves. Mason jars of a yellowish liquid lined the walls. Slocum took one down, broke off the top, and took a deep whiff. He recoiled.

"White lightning," he muttered. The Terwilligers could weather any twister if they drank enough of the potent 'shine. He made certain to hold the match far away from the volatile liquid he had spilled over his hand.

With the light fading as the match burned down, he made another quick turn and made sure he saw all the corners of the small cellar. There wasn't any evidence anyone had been here in weeks. Reluctantly climbing back up the ladder, he emerged into the sultry night and looked at the sky. The stars were so bright he could see easily, but the one thing he couldn't see was what the outlaws had done with the two little girls.

He made his way back to the house. Wilson had cut away his pant leg and worked to clean the wound.

"Damned trap had rusty teeth," he said. "Found a bottle of moonshine and poured it on the cut. Burned like hell but I think I made sure nothing's going to kill me."

"Not unless you drink that liquid shit," Slocum said. "If you need more, I found a cellar full of it."

Wilson looked hard at him in the darkness.

"But no Yarrow girls?"

"I want to look around when the sun comes up. I suppose I ought to drag the bodies out, but damned if I am going to bury them."

"Put 'em in the storm cellar and close the door," the soldier suggested.

"Ought to put them down there and set fire to their 'shine."

"Don't see a problem with that." Wilson got to his feet and stretched his injured leg. "I'll be good as new 'fore you know it." He looked again at Slocum and finally said, "I don't know where else to look."

"We should have dogged their trail. *I* should have." Slocum frowned, then said, "They had a dog."

"The Terwilligers? I doubt it. They were worse than Apaches about dogs. Hated them."

"The Yarrows had a dog. Windmill. If the Terwilligers took the girl, the dog wouldn't just run off."

"They'd have shot it on the spot," Wilson said, "since they hated dogs so much."

"Windmill would have protected the girls." Slocum perched on the edge of a table that barely supported his weight. "We need to look around the Yarrow farm harder."

He cursed himself for not doing so when he had shaken

off the effects of having his head all bashed in. Thinking straight had been a problem, but he couldn't use that as an excuse for simply riding to Fort Stockton to get troopers on the Terwilligers' trail. He should have looked harder.

"No sense beatin' up on yourself, Slocum. We'll find out the truth soon enough, 'less you want to ride all night."

They reached the Yarrow farm by sunrise.

Sergeant Wilson was asleep in the saddle and Slocum was in hardly better condition. Both were driven by the need to find out what happened to the little girls. If the Terwilligers hadn't spirited them off, there had to be another explanation. At least Slocum hoped there was. They had searched the spread the best they could but a churning in his gut persisted. Had they missed something? The Terwilligers weren't clever men, but they had been at their thievery and mopery for a lot of years. They might have accidentally found a way to hide the girls that had escaped two tired men on their trail.

Slocum touched his six-shooter and knew the soldier had been right. He was too quick, too good with the pistol. If he had missed or just winged Pa Terwilliger, they might have found out what had happened here.

Looking around the Yarrow farm didn't give him any good feeling that they would succeed in their hunt. Rain during the night had further wiped away tracks in the dirt, if there had been much chance of finding the proper trail before the storm that had pelted them with small hail and cold, wet drops for more than an hour.

Wilson's horse came to a halt, but the sergeant didn't wake up. He snored loudly and wove from side to side. He had long ago learned the trooper's trick of sleeping in the saddle. Slocum was loath to wake him, though it might be good for the injured soldier to lie down inside the farmhouse. His leg had swollen up to twice its normal size. Slocum had lanced it to drain the pus, and that had helped keep

Wilson in the saddle. If gangrene set in, chopping off the leg was about all Slocum could think to do. They were too far from Gregory or the fort to get the sergeant to a doctor before that drastic surgery would be needed.

Movement at the corner of his eye caused Slocum to jerk around. At first he didn't see what had alerted him. He looked across the yard, where chickens had once pecked away at bits of grain Mrs. Yarrow had tossed out for them. Nothing here. He slowly lifted his gaze to the edge of a plowed field and saw a dark shape fading away.

"Wilson! Stay here!"

Slocum heard the sergeant grunt and jerk upright, but he was already galloping toward the field. Whoever he had seen was too large for a young girl. It might be nothing more than a shadow caused by an animal caught in the rising sun, but Slocum's instincts told him differently. He reached the field and the spot where he had seen the movement. In the rain-soft earth were clear boot prints, freshly made and undoubtedly left by the man who worked hard not to be seen.

Riding slowly down the rows of struggling corn, Slocum warily watched for any movement to betray the man he pursued. The sound of a galloping horse told him he was headed in the wrong direction. He cut across the rows and broke out into a cleared, unplowed field in time to see a rider disappear down a draw. In hot pursuit, Slocum rode until his paint began to falter. The old horse had held up well under all Slocum had asked of it the last week or so, but such a burst of speed taxed it past endurance.

It stumbled, forcing Slocum to slow. He finally brought the gelding to a halt. Ahead, outlined against the dawn sky, sat a rider, watching, unmoving. Then the horse reared, front hooves clawing at the air in Slocum's direction. The rider wheeled about and disappeared over the ridge.

Slocum seethed at losing the man so easily. He didn't force the paint but allowed it to pick its own pace as he crested the hill. The mysterious rider was nowhere to be seen. His tracks were plain, but following them on a tired horse was out of the question, especially when Slocum worried about Sergeant Wilson and his leg.

And the Yarrow girls. That was a puzzle that had to be solved before he went thundering across the prairie after a will-o'-the-wisp.

"Let's go back. There has to be some fodder in the barn for you," Slocum said, patting the horse's neck. The paint responded with more strength than Slocum thought remained in the exhausted animal's body. It understood that food and rest awaited it in the Yarrows' barn.

It took close to a half hour to thread his way back and get the horse to a stall. The amount of grain for fodder was sparse but better than the paint was likely to get otherwise. Slocum put it into a nosebag, curried the horse, and made sure it had water before going to the ranch house. Wilson's horse stood patiently tethered outside the front door.

Slocum took the steps two at a time and went into the house. Wilson had flopped out on the sofa. His half-closed eyelids fluttered and came fully open when Slocum stopped a few feet from him. The soldier had his pistol on the sofa beside him.

"Wondered where you'd got off to. Find anything?"

"Somebody's been dogging our trail," Slocum said. "He was hiding out in the cornfield, but I lost him."

"Horse's tired, too," Wilson said, understanding the problem immediately. "We all need rest 'fore gettin' on back to the post."

"Fort Stockton's not going anywhere. We can rest until you're up to the trip."

"Want to look around here, too. Must be some clues what happened to the girls."

"Rest up. I'll get you something to eat, if there's anything in the larder."

Wilson made some incoherent reply and leaned back. This time his eyes closed entirely. His breathing became shallow but regular. Slocum wasn't afraid of having the soldier die on him anytime soon. Like all good troopers, Wilson had learned how to take his rest when and where possible.

Slocum went into the small kitchen and began opening cabinets. He found some food but most of the containers were empty. A discarded flour sack by the back door caught his attention. He knelt and picked it up. A tiny white cloud cascaded to the floor where damp spots showed how the rain the night before had blown under the door.

The flour sack had been dropped recently, maybe only minutes before he and Wilson had ridden to the farm.

Thought of the stranger spying on them came to mind, but Slocum wasn't convinced the man was a squatter living here now that the rightful owners were gone. If he had camped inside the house for any length of time, there'd be signs. A quick tour through the house showed the bedclothes rumpled but not likely to have been slept on recently.

Slocum stared when he reached an even smaller room, obviously the girls' bedroom. The blankets had been taken off the bed and were nowhere to be seen.

"Wilson?" He went into the front room, but the soldier was sound asleep. Even waking him for food seemed against the laws of nature. He needed rest more than anything else.

Slocum returned to the kitchen and opened the door. It took him a few seconds to find the carefully hidden tracks—and when he did, he saw right away they weren't human. His heart beat faster as he stepped out into the morning sun and looked in the direction of the barn. The tracks were plainly visible halfway there.

He went into the yard, dropped to his hands and knees, and sighted along the ground to find the ridges left by the animal paws. Straightening, he saw they went into the stand of trees some distance from the house. Yarrow had built his house here to use those trees as a windbreak as the gusts usually whipped up from the southlands. Now Slocum knew they held something more in the way of protection.

Stride long, not bothering to follow the animal's tracks, he went into the woods and looked around to get his bearings. He had been in here once before and damned himself for not coming here sooner.

Before he could call out, he heard a growl that meant a dog was ready for a fight. Slocum put his hand on his six-shooter but did not draw.

"You know me, Windmill. You don't have to protect the girls from me."

The snarling dog crouched low in the bushes, fangs showing, eyes narrowed for the attack.

"Audrey, Claudia!" He called out loud enough to be heard but not so loud that he would spook them—he hoped. "It's me, John Slocum. I've come back looking for you. Sergeant Wilson and I'll take you to Fort Stockton."

Windmill hunkered down even more, then coiled, ready to launch an attack. It was a mangy dog, scrawny and hardly worth notice, but it was protecting the girls and would fight to the death.

"I don't want to hurt Windmill. I'd back off, but he'll attack if I do. I don't want to shoot him."

"Mr. Slocum, don't hurt him!"

"Hush, Claudia. Be quiet!" came the immediate admonishment.

"Your ma and pa are dead. The men who killed them are dead now, too. Sergeant Wilson and I made sure of that."

"Who were they?"

He couldn't tell which of the girls spoke, but he thought it was the older one, Audrey.

"A clan of no-accounts named Terwilliger. They have— had—a spread a dozen miles west of here. We thought they had kidnapped you. Glad to find they haven't."

He kept his eyes on the dog. The hindquarters quivered

from the strain of being tensed, but the lips relaxed a mite and Windmill didn't growl quite as deep in his throat. When the two girls appeared from the brush, the dog fell down to his belly in relief and barked. This time it was a friendly, greeting bark and not one of warning.

"The sergeant's hurt bad," Slocum said. "He stepped in a trap the Terwilligers set. Either of you know anything about how to doctor a bad cut?"

The two girls exchanged looks, then the younger one smiled almost shyly and said, "I do. Sorta. Ma showed me when Audrey got all cut up last fall."

"The sergeant would appreciate it if you could help him clean his wound and see to it being tended. I'm not sure I did it right."

Slocum saw that his approach worked wonders. The two girls hugged each other, then ran to him, each taking a hand in their own and pulling him behind them as they raced to the house. Windmill dashed around as if herding sheep, more playful now.

"Look who I found, Sergeant," Slocum said. The soldier's eyes fluttered open. When he saw the girls, a smile broke out like the rising sun.

"Glad to see you young ladies."

"Boil some water," Claudia said, enjoying that she could boss her older sister around.

"I'll help," Slocum said, wanting to talk with the girl. Let Wilson engage Claudia awhile.

"I know how to boil water," Audrey said primly.

"I'll start a fire for you." As Slocum worked, he asked, "I saw a man prowling around in the field. You know who it was?"

"We saw him a couple times. Claudia and I hid. It was all we could do to keep Windmill from going after him, but we wouldn't let him. The man was scary."

"You get a good look at his face?"

"No. He always seemed to stand in shadow or be looking away from us. All I can say is that he wore a gray shirt with a long tear along the back. Up here." She stretched around and pointed to her left shoulder. "It might have just been a seam that came unsewed, but I think it was tore. Might be he rode through the thicket hunting for us and caught it on a twig."

"He might be the man I'm hunting," Slocum said, wondering if Beatrice Sampson would recognize the description as being that of her brother.

Or was it another outlaw looking for an easy score?

Slocum got the fire blazing in the iron stove, slammed the door, and stepped back. Audrey heaved a kettle onto the top and said in a low voice, "We saw the graves. You buried Mama and Papa?"

"I did. Sergeant Wilson and I did."

"You said words over them? Like a preacher? Mama would have wanted that."

"That's not something I do," Slocum said. He rushed on, saying, "But the sergeant did. They were pretty words."

"He's a nice man."

Slocum said nothing more as they waited for the water to boil. When it did, Audrey soaked some rags in the water, then carried them into the front room, where her sister had peeled back the field bandage Slocum had put on the leg wound.

"They're fixing me up real good, Slocum," Wilson said. Their eyes locked. To the girls, the soldier said, "We have to go back to Fort Stockton. You have any relatives?"

The girls both started sniffling, giving the answer more eloquently than words ever could.

"The missus and me, we lost our children. For a while, you want to stay with us? If something better comes up, you could go on. A relative might find you and—"

Sergeant Wilson found himself surrounded by sobbing

little girls. Slocum stepped out onto the porch where Windmill sat, head cocked to one side and ears alert. Slocum followed the dog's line of sight and saw in the distance the rider he had spotted before.

He might, just might, be wearing a gray shirt. Then he was gone.

10

"I'll let you go the rest of the way," Slocum said, seeing the low wall around Fort Stockton and the sentry pacing out his station. It would only be a few minutes before the guard spotted them and raised the alarm.

"The captain won't eat you alive."

"That's what I'm afraid of," Slocum said. "Likely, he'd shoot me and then serve me up for dinner. You go on in. You can explain everything that's happened."

"I shouldn't be the one taking all the credit," Wilson said. He shifted in the saddle and winced. The girls had done a right fine job of patching him up but the wound would take another couple weeks to heal properly before he wasn't in pain.

"You can do all the explaining," Slocum said, inclining his head in the direction of the two girls trampling along valiantly with Windmill at their heels. They had ridden behind the two men most of the way, but Slocum didn't want to be hindered if he had to hightail it away from the post. His reception from Captain Legrange hadn't been good on the best of occasions. Finding out about the Terwilligers' deaths wouldn't likely gall him, but Slocum's part as a civilian and how he had rescued Wilson would all make for a long explanation he wanted to avoid.

And there was the rider who always seemed to stay a mile or two off. Slocum had caught sight of the man less than an hour before. If Wilson and the Yarrow girls continued into the fort, he might have a chance to nab the man or at least get a better look at his face.

"You're making a mountain out of a molehill, Slocum," the soldier said. "But you got to come back by in a week or two to see how things are going."

"A family's what they need right now." Slocum wondered how Wilson's wife would react to having a brood underfoot again. It might be just what the woman needed—or it might be poison for both her and the girls. Considering all that Audrey and Claudia had gone through, he hoped they fit into the Wilson household just fine. They needed more family than a dog, even one as good as Windmill.

"You planning on getting the drop on the man shadowing us?"

"Can't put anything past you," Slocum said. "When I get back in a couple weeks, I suspect I'll find you're wrapped around the fingers of three women." He waved to the girls, who had finally narrowed the distance, then wheeled his horse about and trotted away.

"Mr. Slocum, don't go!"

"Got to do my job and deliver some more mail," he called out. Then he put his head down and pushed his paint for all the horse could give. A ravine running parallel to the fort gave him some shelter from direct view and took him in the desired direction.

When he had ridden a couple miles, he urged his horse up a steep embankment overlooking a level stretch of prairie. He bit his lip to keep from crying out in glee. His trick had worked. He was less than a hundred yards from the rider.

The rider who wore a gray shirt.

The man was looking away, but something alerted him to Slocum's presence. He put his head down and glanced back over his left shoulder. As he did, part of the shirt opened up and showed bare flesh. While there might be two men on the range with gray shirts, Slocum doubted there were two matching the description given by the Yarrow girls. But now that he had been spotted, Slocum knew he was in for a race.

The man lit out like his horse's tail had been set on fire. He galloped hard and fast. Slocum urged the paint to as much speed as he could, but the horse was old and tired. The distance between Slocum and his pursuer slowly widened and then the man evaporated, gone from sight in less than a heartbeat.

When Slocum rode to the spot where he had last seen the man, he saw what had happened. He had snuck up on his quarry using a deep ravine cut by the recent rains. The rider had done the same thing to escape. Slocum eased his horse to the muddy ravine bottom and soon saw how hard it would be tracking anyone. The inch or two of water left in the ravine from the recent rains covered hoofprints in the mud. As the sluggishly flowing water moved southward, even the small traces were erased.

He rode his paint to the bank and looked in both directions, but the rider might have gone a ways, then hidden.

Slocum's dejection soon faded as he turned to find the road meandering away from Fort Stockton. He had mail to deliver—and had proven to his satisfaction that the man after him was no hallucination. Who he might be or what he wanted could be settled later. Now that he had revealed himself, he was no longer a bogeyman.

An hour later, Slocum used the map Underwood had given him to find the road and a signpost that had been blown over. He had to dismount to scrape away the mud, then wondered which way the sign had pointed. He was near a town, but which direction? Seeing another sign a hundred yards farther, Slocum rode to it and read the name.

He fished around in the mail bags until he found a small package for Justin Framingham. Holding the package at arm's length, he double-checked the name. It matched the one on the sign.

The road leading across the prairie in the direction of the Framingham farm had been washed out in a dozen places, forcing Slocum to detour often as he rode the mile or more back to the farmhouse. He drew rein and stared at the destruction. The twister had bounced along here and had plucked away the roof and the north side of the house, leaving the rest standing. All around evidence of the incredible destruction caused by the tornado made him wonder if anyone could have survived.

He touched the package with Framingham's name on it, wondering if he ought to return it to Underwood or simply toss it onto the pile of debris.

Slocum rode forward slowly. His paint shied, telling him bodies were buried under the debris. He might not see them, but the horse smelled them. Its nostrils went wide and its eyes showed white all around.

"Whoa, easy now," he said, gentling the horse. It refused to be mollified and started backing away.

Bowing to the inevitable, Slocum let the horse get far enough away that it was no longer spooked. He dismounted, tethered the horse to a wagon wheel that had recently been part of a wagon, if the grease around the hub was any indication. Where the wagon had blown, he couldn't say. Nowhere in sight.

He returned to the house, his steps slow and his eyes peeled for any trace of a body. He was getting tired of burying victims. Gregory had been half destroyed, and he had counted himself lucky not to be on the burial detail there with Old George and the telegrapher. But the Yarrows had been murdered by outlaws. He had no compunction about letting their killers rot on the prairie, feed for buzzards and bugs.

But here was another matter. He was used to violence, even mindless violence such as the Terwilligers dished out. The starkness of the twister's destruction was completely impersonal. Nothing could have withstood the fierce tornado winds or the blinding rain and hailstorm surrounding it. Men killing men he understood. This was destruction on a scale that made him both humble and angry.

Before it no one stood for long. Not even John Slocum.

He closed his eyes and remembered the helpless feeling when the twister had lifted the rear of the stagecoach into the air and sent him flying. The fastest gun, the strongest arm, the quickest run, all meant nothing against the tornado.

His hand flashed to his six-shooter when he heard faint sounds from under the house's wreckage. He took his hand away when he realized it was only wind blowing between planks, causing a whistling sound that he had thought to be human.

Slocum made his way into the tumble of planks and furniture. As he pawed through, not sure what he sought, he had to stop and shake his head when he saw a large mirror on a dresser. Rain had smeared mud across the flat surface, but the mirror hadn't even been nicked, much less broken. In the middle of such destruction, the tornado had chosen to leave this untouched.

He rubbed off some of the dirt and looked at his reflection. It was a good mirror. It'd be a shame to leave it out here, but he had no way of returning to Fort Stockton with it. Such a large looking glass would fetch a decent price and help Audrey and Claudia, just a little. As he turned, movement behind caused him to go into a crouch, spin, and whip out his six-gun.

The Colt Navy centered on a disheveled woman holding a shovel. She looked at him—or did she look *through* him?

He wasn't sure she even realized he stood in the middle of the destroyed house staring at what was likely her mirror.

"Ma'am, you Miz Framingham?"

He repeated his question before she snapped away from whatever consumed her thoughts. Her eyes focused on him for the first time.

"Who are you?"

"Name's Slocum. Came to deliver a package to Justin Framingham."

"He's dead."

"You his wife?" The woman nodded dully. "Then I reckon you can take this in his stead." Slocum held out the brown-paper-wrapped package. "I'm not the regular mailman."

"Usually drive into Gregory for our mail."

"Not much of the town left, ma'am," he said. "Postmaster's dead and I was out of a job as stage driver so I agreed to bring the mail around." He wasn't sure why he felt he had to explain. It might have been nothing more than filling the silence when she didn't respond as he'd expected.

"I buried him. My husband. I buried him."

"The tornado?"

She looked hard at him, then nodded solemnly.

"I didn't want to. I loved Justin. Most of the time." She looked around, her shock returning. "This was our place."

Slocum made his way through the rubble to stand near her.

"That's a mighty fine mirror. The wind didn't even crack it."

"It came from Boston. A wedding present from my pa and ma."

"It survived. You can, too," he said softly.

She dropped the shovel and threw herself into his arms. Slocum held her clumsily. She was quite an armful, young and pretty under the dirt. He didn't know what to do, so he held her close until her sobbing slowed and finally stopped.

"That wasn't very mature of me," she said.

"You've had a big loss. Any others in your family besides your husband?"

"No," she said. She clung to him, no matter how he tried to disengage. Slocum finally surrendered to the inevitable and let her hang on. She mumbled something into his shoulder.

"What's that, ma'am?"

"My name's Bonnie and . . . and I need to forget. Make me forget all this. For a while."

She looked up at him, her lips slightly parted, waiting to be kissed. Her body trembled against his as he asked, "Are you sure this is the right thing to do?"

She kissed him with a passion that caused him to recoil. She followed his lips with hers. Her fingers clutched fiercely at his arms, keeping him from backing away any farther.

When she broke off, she whispered hoarsely, "Please. I won't ask anything else from you. The death. I . . . I want to feel alive, to not think about all this for a little while. Please."

Slocum looked around and saw that a mattress had been tossed away from the bedsprings—which he didn't see anywhere. The side of the mattress had been ripped open, leaking wads of stuffing out onto a pile of rubble. She saw it same time he did and turned so that she could fall backward onto it. As she fell, her fingers curled like hooks into his upper arms, pulling him down atop her.

She looked up. Her lips moved in a silent plea. "Please."

This time he kissed her. Her arms wrapped around his neck and pulled him down hard against her softly yielding body. Beneath him she began wiggling, moving, her legs positioning themselves. He reached down and fumbled to get his gun belt off and cast aside. Then her fingers joined his trying to pop the fly buttons.

He wasn't hard when she dug into his jeans and found his penis. She needed him, but he wasn't sure he could deliver. Then her fingers curled around his limpness and began squeezing, not with brutal necessity but gentle persuasion. In spite of his doubts, Slocum felt himself growing harder. When she pulled him out from his jeans, he was firm in her grasp.

"Do it," she said. "Please. I need to feel more than I do now. Make me feel everything. Make me feel . . . nothing."

She reached down and hiked her skirts, bunching them up around her waist. She arched her back and lifted her rump off the mattress to aid him. It took Slocum a bit longer to unfasten the ties holding her undergarments, but he finally pulled them down around her thighs to expose the dark, furred triangle between her legs.

His hand pressed down. She closed her eyes and moaned at his manual manipulation. His fingers slipped up and down her nether lips until juices oozed from within. He smeared this oil around the upper juncture of her vee'd sex lips. The tiny pink spire rising there quivered under his touch. He stroked back and forth, flicking it with his thumb.

The woman gasped, lifted her hips, and pressed her crotch into his palm. When his finger slid easily into her tightness, she cried out in release.

"Yes, I need more, more, please, oh please, more!"

She thrashed about beneath him, then gripped his fleshy stalk and pulled insistently toward the spot where his finger still moved in small circles. He pulled his hand away and inserted himself. For a moment, neither moved. Then Slocum found himself astride a bucking bronco. She lifted and twisted, dropped and rotated her hips, demanding ever more from him. He slid in and out of her heated center and then gave himself over to the obvious. Clutching her shoulders, he rolled over, pulling her with him.

They remained locked together at the waist, but she came out on top, straddling his waist. He looked up into her drawn face. He wasn't sure this was passion rather than grim determination—and it didn't matter. She shoved her hands down on his chest, lifted herself up, and then slammed down hard, taking him balls deep into her clutching sheath.

She began moving with greater speed and determination until she set a pace Slocum was hard pressed to match. Finally, he stopped. He simply lay back and let her pleasure herself. His shaft burned with the friction of the fierce up and down moves, her rotating hips, the way she threw her head back as if she rode a wild stallion. Faster she moved and then he groaned as she tightened around his buried length, making him think he would be crushed to death.

A long, loud cry rose to the heavens and then she fell forward, her cheek resting next to his. He felt hot tears flowing again, but this time when he held her, the tenseness was gone from her body. He wasn't sure how long they lay there, but the sun dipped low in the west when she finally sat up.

She looked at him as if he were a total stranger, stood, and arranged her skirts.

"Can we leave now?" she asked. "There is nothing keeping me here, and I would prefer to live at Fort Stockton, or perhaps at Gregory."

"If you don't mind traveling in the dark," he said. She turned away as he tucked himself back into his jeans and buttoned up. He stood, looked around for his holster, and bent to retrieve it.

"I want to be away from here as fast as I possibly can go."

The bullet tore through her chest, staggered her back a pace, and then she fell heavily.

11

For an instant Slocum froze. He remained bent over, hand on his holster and eyes on the fallen woman. He heard nothing but the report echoing away to nothing. He doubted the shooter had a good view of him in the twilight, but Slocum couldn't be sure. Slowly sinking to his knees to avoid quick movement that might draw unwanted attention, he drew his six-shooter and then worked his way toward the woman.

Her sightless eyes stared upward at the evening star hovering at the horizon. She wasn't going to make a wish on that first star or any other one. She had been killed instantly with a bullet through the heart.

Slocum doubted the sniper was that good a shot, but lucky was sometimes better that skillful. Or had the unseen gunman wanted to kill Bonnie Framingham? A more likely explanation caused a chill to seize Slocum. He might have been the target and the shooter had missed in the gathering darkness.

He moved as quietly as he could until he got behind a heap of debris. Part of the house's wall still stood. He edged upward and peered through what had been a window in the direction of the shot. If the dark protected him from sight, it worked similarly for the gunman. Try as he might, Slocum couldn't see movement from where the shot had been fired.

Ducking back, he looked around, then made his way along the broken wall. A quick look around it didn't draw fire. Staying low, he made his way to a well, then to a pile of bent metal that once had been a plow and was now driven into the ground by the tornado. He took a deep breath, then ran for all he was worth toward a stock tank.

Still no fire.

He pressed his back against the earthen tank, then oozed over the top into the muddy bottom and made his way to the far side. This time he drew fire when he poked his head up. The foot-long orange muzzle flash pinpointed the man's location. Slocum tried to remember what the terrain between the two of them looked like. He hadn't gotten a good look when he had ridden up, and after that, he had been too occupied. At least the woman's last wish had been granted. She had forgotten her woes for a brief moment and then the bullet had taken her to the Promised Land.

Slocum went to the side of the stock tank, slithered over its side, and fell to the ground. From here he worked his way along on his belly until he reached an outbuilding. Here he got to his feet, put his thumb on the pistol's hammer, and spun around, firing as rapidly as he could at the place where he had seen the muzzle flash.

He intended to drive the man from cover or force him to return fire. Slocum knew he was a sitting duck out in the open, with his own muzzle flashes and reports pinpointing him in the dark. Four of his slugs tore through some brush. Then he listened hard.

Nothing.

Running forward, aware he had only two rounds left in the cylinder, he bulled through the brush to the other side. The mud didn't hold footprints very well but what he saw on the ground were fresh. He bent to examine one, but the loose soil and water robbed the print of any real information. He found a rifle casing and tucked it into a vest pocket. Then he pressed on into the dark.

Twenty minutes later, he admitted defeat. He hadn't heard the sniper ride off, but there was no trace to be found. The woman might as well have been killed by a ghost in the night.

As he returned to the wrecked house, he tried to piece everything together and decided there wasn't a good answer. He might have been the intended target. Or it could have been Bonnie Framingham. For all he knew, the lack of visibility might have confused the shooter into thinking husband and wife stood amid the ruins of their house. Justin Framingham might have enemies galore, as many as the Terwilligers. There was no way Slocum could know.

He retrieved his gun belt and took the time to reload the four spent chambers. Strapping on the cross-draw holster made him feel better, even if the sight of the woman's body didn't. Poking around until he found the shovel she had held, he knew what had to be done next. He used several matches, finding where she had buried her husband. Slocum dug a grave alongside and did the best he could for a marker.

Sergeant Wilson had said words over the Yarrows' graves, but Slocum didn't know Bonnie Framingham any more than he had the Yarrows and wasn't inclined to false words.

He did the best he could, saying, "I'll find who shot you down. That I promise." With that he threw down the shovel, turned his back to the grave, and walked away. Delivering mail wasn't proving to be a job he did all that well.

His nervous paint balked when he mounted but soon enough decided getting away from the wreckage and death was better than fighting its rider. Slocum rode for an hour, camped under the stars, then found the road at daybreak and made it into Gregory within the hour.

The sound of hammers and saws made Slocum come alert. The townspeople worked industriously to rebuild the half of the town that had been devastated. In another week Gregory would be restored to prestorm splendor.

Slocum snorted at the idea the people rebuilt to have their town leveled again by a new storm. That was reality out here on the plains. Where would the citizens move that was any better? The town supplied Fort Stockton, acted as a junction for the stage line, and rumors abounded about the railroad, even if many didn't believe it would happen—and would eventually kill off the town when the line bypassed Gregory. The entire state would be connected with the steel rails one day. There would be winners and losers, the losers turning to ghost towns in a few months.

Slocum knew the stagecoach would be the first casualty. Why ship passengers or mail in a creaking stage pulled by a team of horses that had to be changed every few miles? The way stations would become ghost towns.

It all seemed futile to him. Better to simply ride on and let others in Gregory worry about becoming relics of the past.

"Hey, Slocum, you done with deliverin' the mail already?" Henry Underwood stepped from the stagecoach office, thumbs hooked into the armholes of his vest. His big belly poked out. For all the destruction in town, he hadn't missed any meals.

"Not sure that's what I want to do with my life," Slocum said, swinging to the ground. He unfastened the mail bags and dropped them in front of the station agent.

"You don't get paid a dime, then. Not for the time you drove the stage, not for nuthin'!"

Underwood obviously thought this threat would bring Slocum around.

"I've seen more than my share of people dying out there," Slocum said. "Sometimes I get to thinking how if I don't see people dying, maybe they won't."

"That's crazy talk. People will die whether you see it or not." Underwood cocked his head to one side and looked hard at Slocum. "Who's been dyin' out there?"

"Captain Legrange told me to mind my own business," Slocum said. That wasn't strictly true but came close enough to the officer's orders.

"He still huntin' for his payroll, I reckon," Underwood said. He rubbed his chin. "There's nuthin' we can do 'bout that. But you *can* deliver the mail."

Slocum thought about the woman who had been cut down after they'd made love. She had been a desperate woman, pushed to the edge and struggling to come back when she had been gunned down for no reason he could tell. The death had shrouded his trail all the way back to town, and he still couldn't figure out if she had been the target or if he had. Even in broad daylight, it would have been a difficult shot for any rifleman.

"I suppose I have things to tell the sheriff."

"No sheriff. Not any longer. He upped and left after he saw what that twister had done to town. He rode around and didn't find things any better elsewhere in Pecos County."

"I saw three people murdered," Slocum said. "Two women and a man, and two little girls left without parents."

"A shame, a real shame," Underwood said, nodding sagely. "That doesn't keep you from deliverin' the mail."

"I'll think about it," Slocum said, taking the reins in hand and starting away.

"Hold on, Slocum. That's the Butterfield Stage Company's horseflesh. It was just loaned to you as an employee on company business."

"You *gave* the horse to me."

"As part of your pay for doin' a job. You don't do the job, you can't keep the horse."

Slocum wrapped the reins around the hitching post.

"I'll think about it," he repeated and walked away, Underwood sputtering behind him. If the stationmaster tried that hard to get him to deliver the mail, Slocum knew it meant that nobody else was available for the job.

He went to a new saloon set up in a tent. The management

hadn't even bothered to scatter sawdust on the ground. The mud came up to the middle of Slocum's boots as he slogged his way to the wood plank laid over two sawhorses.

Behind the bar were a half-dozen whiskey bottles and a keg of beer.

"Welcome," the barkeep said. His boots caused a sucking sound with every step he took. The ground wasn't in any better shape behind the rude bar than it was in front. "What kin I git you?"

Slocum searched his pockets and came up with a dime. He dropped it on the bar, where it rolled about and finally came to rest after ringing hollowly.

"Beer, till that runs out."

The barkeep laughed and put a mug with frothy beer in front of him.

"That just does cover the cost, mister. Ain't gettin' supplies in 'cuz of the tornado damage. Been told it'll be a week before anything comes in from San Angelo. That means cases of whiskey and new kegs of beer."

"Twister destroyed the old saloon?"

"One of 'em was on the wrong side of the street. The other one, that was sittin' pretty, well, the owner upped and left. Took all his stock with him. Don't know what happened, but it's a fact of life. Me, I was lucky. I'd got so drunk I was passed out in a ditch when the twister hit. Went right on over me, or so they tell me."

"You own this place?"

"Just work here. Me, I'd have a classier joint. I'd have a mirror behind the bar." The man laughed and slogged off to serve another customer.

Slocum looked around the tent. Four chairs at a table constituted all the furniture. The walls flapped noisily in the wind, and the stench from smoke and dirty bodies was enough to put Slocum off his feed. Men didn't come here to socialize as much as they did to knock back the suddenly expensive booze. Slocum considered finding someone with a wagon and offering to drive back supplies from San Angelo or Buena Vista. Whoever had goods to sell would become rich mighty fast.

A single load of whiskey would give both the town and the fort a needed boost—and also deliver a huge profit to the man selling it.

He sipped his beer until not even foam remained. Other than finding someone needing a teamster, all Slocum could think to keep body and soul together was to deliver mail for Underwood. The old paint was a sorry animal, going deaf and not a little bit on the balky side, but he had come to appreciate the horse's heart. Even exhausted, it had kept putting one hoof in front of the other to keep moving.

Stepping out into the main street, he looked around and immediately saw a white handkerchief fluttering to catch his attention. Slocum wasn't sure he was up to dealing with Beatrice Sampson. It quickly became apparent he either turned and ran or spoke with her. She hurried across the street in his direction, coming at him like a Sioux warrior intent on counting coup.

"I didn't know you were back, John," she said, stopping a few feet away and staring up at him. Her breasts rose and fell heavily from the exertion of running so far. He remembered how their other exertion had caused a different kind of excitement in her. She wasn't a bad-looking woman, but he couldn't help comparing her needs with those of the woman he had just buried.

"Been out riding circuit, delivering mail. Or trying to."

"Did you," she said, lowering her voice and stepping closer, "see *him*?"

"Your brother?" Slocum considered this. There had to be a reason the rider following him had turned so deadly. At least once he had been shot at, and an innocent woman had died. "Might be we crossed paths. Can't rightly say since I've never gotten close enough to ask."

"He'd never talk to you. He's crazy."

"How crazy?"

Beatrice's eyes widened at his question.

"Murdering crazy. He has to be brought in. Or put in the ground before he does something terrible."

"Might be he's done that, and the law around here doesn't much care." He spat a gob of dust that had formed on his lip where beer foam had accumulated. "What there is of the law."

"The sheriff is gone, I know," she said. "That makes it all the more serious about Joshua."

"What does Captain Legrange have to say on the matter?"

"He . . . he's in command of Fort Stockton now. All the other officers are gone. Dead, likely, but certainly not reporting back."

Slocum considered this. Legrange would have his hands full if most of the soldiers were missing. For command to come down to him, several officers had to be missing. Maybe a half dozen. The tornado had done more than destroy houses and lives. It had severely affected the Army's ability to patrol the area.

"He's worried about Indians, but there's so much else to concern him," she said.

"Wants his payroll, more 'n likely," Slocum said.

"Never mind the captain and his problems, John. You have to do something about Joshua."

"What's he wearing?"

"His clothing?" The question took Beatrice by surprise. "I don't know. Clothes. Nothing special. Jeans, a shirt."

"What color?"

"I think he was wearing a gray shirt last time I saw him, but I don't remember. So much was happening that—"

"He's the one that tried to gun me down," Slocum said.

"No! John, he's dangerous. If he'd wanted you dead, he would have succeeded."

Slocum said nothing to her about the obvious lack of

confidence in his abilities. Still, she had a point. Joshua had all the time in the world to lay his ambush and commit yet another murder. If Beatrice was right, her brother had shot down her husband during the stagecoach robbery. From the distance and accuracy shown, he was one hell of a marksman. Slocum had ridden open fields and along roads where a sniper could make an easy twenty-yard shot and never be seen yet he was still alive. Whatever drove Joshua to kill was indeed beyond Slocum's ken.

"Did you know a woman named Bonnie Framingham? Lived maybe fifteen miles outside of town with her husband, Justin."

Beatrice shook her head.

"The name doesn't sound familiar. We moved here a while back, but meeting people in town proved a chore. We were outsiders. Those who lived farther out, well, we never got a chance to meet any of them. Not that I remember, at least."

Slocum heard something less than the truth in her words but wasn't inclined to find out what Beatrice lied about.

"I'm not able to do any hunting for your brother, unless he's in town."

"Why?"

"I lost my horse." He looked across the street. Underwood had already taken the paint and put it into the corral behind the depot.

"Did Joshua steal it?" Beatrice looked at him in wide-eyed surprise. "I can't believe that."

"I don't have a horse or gear," Slocum said. "It'll take me a spell to get a mount and a saddle."

"I . . . I can give you money. You can buy something. This is *so* important to me, John. I can't tell you how important it is that you stop Joshua."

"You want him dead?"

"I want him brought in so he can be helped. There's a madhouse down around Austin, or so I hear. If he's locked up there, he won't hurt anyone else. And . . . and if you shoot him, that might be the best for all of us. Especially Joshua. He is a sad man."

Sad and crazy. Slocum wondered how much more she would tell him about her brother. From what little he had learned asking around town, the Sampsons were almost hermits, staying to themselves. They hadn't even gone to barn dances or church socials, preferring their own company. Some folks were like that. He wondered about Beatrice's husband. And her brother. And her.

"I might find you a suitable horse," she said, as if coming to a hard decision. "I can't give it to you, but you are free to use it if you are tracking down my brother."

She took his arm and steered him along the street. The sounds of hammers falling on nails and the scent of sawdust from newly sawed planks filled his ears and nose. Beatrice rambled on, and he ignored her as he turned over everything she had said, wondering why he was involved at all. Being the driver on that ill-fated stage had something to do with it, but he owed her nothing if her brother had killed her husband. There might not be any lawmen left in town, but she was cozy enough with Captain Legrange to persuade him to send out a patrol. One or two men rather than a squad might be all it took to bring Joshua to justice.

"There's a livery. I know the owner and can make a deal. What do you need?"

"I never said I'd go hunting for your brother."

"But, John, you must! I . . . I feel he is nearing the point where he will be uncontrollable. He'll start killing at random."

"Might be doing that now," he said.

"You *have* to stop him. If not for me, then for all the innocents he might slaughter."

They went into the livery stable, but no one was around. Slocum looked over the horses and any would do. Any of them was better than the old paint, but he had no idea if any of these had the heart of that other horse.

"Here," she said, pressing a wad of greenbacks into his hand. "Buy what you need."

"The owner's not here."

"John!" She shrieked and pointed. "There. At the window. It was Joshua!"

He dropped the wad of scrip as his hand flashed to his six-shooter, but he didn't draw. He had seen nothing, not even a shadow moving across the sunlit pane.

"I'm not imagining it. I saw him. You have to stop him, John. Now, please, for me, please!"

"Stay here," he said, crossing the stable in three quick strides so he could peer out the window. He didn't see anyone outside.

With a grunt, he pulled up the window and climbed through, careful where he put his feet. Boot prints came to the window and then left. Someone had been here, but had it been Joshua? The livery stable had to bring customers in all day long, and for all he knew, the tracks belonged to the missing owner.

He drew his pistol and held it at his side as he followed the clear trail leading from the stable. The tracks turned and went into an alley. From here whoever had made the prints had gone to the main street. Slocum ran to the middle of the street and looked in both directions, hunting a man wearing a gray shirt with a tear along the left shoulder. All he saw was industry as the citizens of Gregory worked to repair the storm damage to their town.

Slocum slid his six-gun back into his holster and returned to the livery stable.

"Couldn't find anyone," he said as he stepped inside. "Beatrice? Where are you?"

He drew his six-shooter again and worked his way slowly down the stalls, searching for the woman.

She was nowhere to be found.

12

It took Slocum a couple seconds to realize something else was missing. The three horses that had been in stalls were gone, too. He backed from the stable and looked at the ground. Outside the door the mud had been churned up, but he couldn't tell if it was recent or had been done an hour earlier. From the sudden disappearance of both Beatrice and the horses, the cut-up ground was recent.

He paced around, trying to find a clearer trail, and thought he saw faint tracks leading directly north out of town. Stewing, he prowled the area like a caged bear, then knew he had to follow the trail. Beatrice might be in real danger—and her brother was the likely reason she had left so fast.

And the three horses had been stolen. Slocum couldn't discount that. If Joshua had ridden in on one, that meant he and Beatrice could swap off as they rode and cover fifty or more miles in a day without running the horses into the ground. As they rode, the others rested. As the horses they were on tired, they switched to the spares. It was an effective way of putting a hell of a lot of miles behind you in a day.

Slocum went back into the stables and pushed around straw on the floor until he found the greenbacks Beatrice had forced into his hand, but without any horses, he might as well wave around a corn stalk. All the money in the world wouldn't buy what didn't exist.

Realizing he had only one way to go after Beatrice and her brother, he reluctantly marched through the middle of town to the depot where Underwood sat on the front porch, pawing through a stack of papers and cursing. The station-master looked up as Slocum approached.

"You can't make me pay you!" Underwood half stood and papers went flying. "Damnation, it's too dark inside and I don't have any kerosene for the lamp and out here the wind catches my papers. I got to file reports or—" Underwood grabbed handfuls of paper and clutched them to his chest. "What is it, Slocum? What do you want?"

"I'll deliver the mail."

Underwood stared at him openmouthed for a moment, then said, "This some kind of trick? You fixin' on stealin' that horse?"

"I can buy the paint." He held out the greenbacks.

Underwood didn't even look at them. He shook his head and began stuffing the papers into his vest as a way to keep the wind from scattering them.

"Not enough. If you ain't seen, horseflesh is at a premium in Gregory after the tornado. But you said you'd deliver the mail? You tellin' the truth?"

Slocum nodded.

"Let me hear you say it. You promise to deliver the mail?"

"I promise. Now let me have the horse and gear. Including the rifle."

"The rifle," Underwood said, as if the notion was foreign to him. "There wasn't a rifle when I sent you out, was there?"

"Do you want me to deliver the damned mail or not?"

"Yes, yes, of course. Nobody in town's got a spare

minute. Every last soul has work to do rebuildin'. You're the only one that don't fit into the community."

"Glad to hear it," Slocum said. He ignored Underwood's demand for an explanation why he'd changed his mind.

He rounded the depot and saw the paint in the corral, contentedly munching some hay. The horse shuddered when it spotted him. Its rest had amounted to only an hour.

Slocum saddled and secured the two canvas mail sacks over the saddlebags, then stepped up. The paint sagged slightly under his weight but otherwise bore up well.

"You get that mail delivered pronto, you hear, Slocum?"

Slocum touched the brim of his hat as he rode past the stationmaster and into the street. He ought to forget about Beatrice and whatever she had gotten mixed up in with her crazy brother. The mail begged to be delivered. Then Slocum remembered the package to Justin Framingham and how that had ended so poorly.

Somebody had killed Bonnie Framingham. Joshua was as likely a candidate for that dishonorable murder as anyone. Slocum turned toward the stables, where the livery owner had returned to find his horses stolen. He waved his arms around and yelled for the marshal, but he finally quieted when he remembered the town didn't have any lawmen.

"You, the driver fellow. You work for Mr. Underwood?"

"I do," Slocum said.

"My horses. They've been took right out from under my nose. Three fine horses. I'm offerin' a ten dollar a head reward for whoever returns them. And I ain't fussy about what happens to the horse thieves what took them!"

"North? Did they head north?"

"How the hell should I know? Go find 'em!" The stable owner began muttering to himself, cursing loud enough now and then for Slocum to overhear.

He turned his paint north and started in the direction he thought Joshua had gone—maybe with Beatrice as his prisoner.

As he rode, Slocum turned over and over the details he knew and tried to understand the bigger motives that Beatrice had kept hidden from him. He had no doubt that she told him only a small part of what drove her brother. Slocum had no idea if Joshua had killed Beatrice's husband or Bonnie Framingham, but it was likely.

Still, something chewed away at him about Bonnie Framingham's death. Slocum had been so close. He might have been the target. Because Beatrice had sent him after her brother? That didn't seem all that likely since Slocum had seen the distant rider paralleling his trail, tracking him, staying just beyond recognition. That horseman knew whom he followed, but did he also know he had missed and killed the distraught woman?

The only way Slocum could get answers was to capture Joshua and ask. He wasn't likely to get the answers easily, but that didn't worry him much. He had learned things from the Apaches that could make a rock cry and a tree beg for mercy. Joshua would tell him what he wanted to know, crazy as a bedbug or not.

The tired paint couldn't go fast but plodded along, more like a plow horse than a saddle-broke horse. Slocum chafed at the slowness of the pace, and when the sky began to darken, he looked around for a decent place to spend the night.

He drew rein and stood in the stirrups when he spotted a flickering orange light not a quarter mile ahead. He took a deep whiff and tried to catch the smoke from the campfire. It was too far off. Slocum wetted his finger and held it high. The wind was blowing from his back toward the campsite. That would carry both sound and scent to anyone at the fire.

Slocum rode at a right angle then cut back to approach the camp from the east, safe from detection because of the gently blowing evening wind. When he was less than a hundred yards away, Slocum dismounted, much to the relief of his horse, then advanced as silently as he could in the dark. Now and then he stepped on a dried twig or brushed against a limb, which caused a soft slithering sound. He hoped the rising wind would cover his sounds. It certainly kept his scent from an alert man.

Closer to the camp, Slocum paused to take in the fire and the dark shapes around it. He might have come upon some cowboys riding the range in search of strays. Or there might be some other reason for pilgrims to be on the trail. The tornado had uprooted too many people.

From his position, Slocum saw two men wrapped in blankets well away from the fire. He frowned when he considered how high the fire was, how far the men were, and how early in the evening it was. His pistol slipped easily into his hand as he advanced. It would take only a few seconds to find out if these were innocent travelers or something more.

"John, it's a trap!"

Beatrice's voice galvanized him. He drove forward hard and fast, flying parallel to the ground and then falling straight down with enough force to knock the wind from his lungs. Gasping for air, he heard the rifle report and hot lead whizzing above him. He wiggled forward, thrusting the gun out to find a target. His grip was a weaker than it ought to have been from his sudden fall, but as he breathed more easily, his strength returned. With it, his eyes cleared.

The dark forms were nothing more than logs wrapped in blankets to dupe him into thinking they were sleeping men. He wasted no time sighting in on either of them. He lifted his sights to a point beyond the fire. A pile of debris looked to be the best spot for the sniper.

"Come on out, Joshua," he called. "I won't shoot you."

He didn't expect Beatrice's brother to surrender. The muzzle flash giving away the man's position was exactly what he had anticipated. His Colt swiveled about and targeted a spot just above the flash. Slocum fired twice, then rolled fast to his right until he fetched up hard against a fallen log. It wouldn't provide any shelter from the return fire, but he only expected to stay there a few seconds.

A couple more rounds sang death in his direction. He got off two more shots and heard a loud grunt. He might have winged Joshua but he doubted it. The man was too well protected by the debris. This was another part of the game, bait dangled out to get him to rise and reveal himself. Slocum waited. Then he fired twice more when he heard a scurrying movement.

He would have gotten to his feet and charged Joshua's position but he took the time to reload. Attacking with an empty six-shooter was a sure way to end up as dead as Bonnie Framingham and all the others Joshua might have murdered.

Slocum moved back in the direction where he had gone to ground originally. A slight depression gave scant cover but he used every bit of the terrain to his advantage as he moved forward. No false promises now. Nothing to give himself away. He came up to the edge of the pile of rubble left by the twister and took a deep, calming breath.

He poked his gun over the top and fired, quickly moving to see if he had hit anything.

Shadows mocked him. If Joshua had been here, he was long gone.

"Beatrice!" Slocum called out, hoping that she would answer. He couldn't see Joshua. He wanted Beatrice to give away her brother's position.

Rising wind gave him his only reply. Turning his head from side to side, he checked in all directions for any sound of movement from humans. He thought he heard scraping noises like someone being dragged along directly north of the camp. Just to be on the safe side, Slocum looked back at the campfire and the two dark shapes there. Neither had moved.

He had to believe they were nothing more than dummies Joshua had used as a lure. This was no time to be foolishly aggressive. He duck walked back to the fire and ripped away the blankets. As he had thought, one was a log and the other a pile of brush. The sides of the blanket had been held down with rocks.

Being so skittish made him angry with himself because it gave Joshua a head start. But he had to be sure nobody was coming up from behind.

He left the camp and circled, gauging where Joshua might have run after failing with his ambush. As he walked, the wind began to pick up, making every footstep more difficult than the last. Dust filled the air and blinded him. When he coughed at a mouthful of dirt, he pulled up his bandanna to cover his nose. This made breathing a sight easier.

Squinting into the wind, he advanced. Barely had he gone twenty yards when the rain began pelting down. It started with a few drops and rapidly escalated into a full-fledged frog strangler. Slocum was forced to pull down the brim of his hat to keep the rain from his eyes.

A swirling column of water surrounded him and almost took his hat off. The rain obliterated any chance he might have had of finding tracks. Worse, he had gotten turned around. His sense of direction, usually good, failed him now as the storm increased in fury.

He yelled, "Joshua!" His cry vanished in the wind's howl. He called out to Beatrice with the same result.

Tracking in the dark was almost impossible, but now he couldn't even light a lucifer to study the ground. The rain turned the dirt into mud. As it fell in heavy sheets, the mud turned to soup. Slocum tucked his gun away, making sure his coat was pulled over it to protect the weapon from the driving rain.

He hunkered down, bent double and facing the ground. He let the heavy rain bounce off his back, but this was only a chance to rest for a moment. Soaked through and through, he was miserable and increasingly uneasy about where Joshua might be. If Beatrice's brother had a whit of sense, he would have run after the ambush and kept running. By now he could be miles away, especially if he had mounted and rode. The rain would catch him in the saddle, but he'd be far from Slocum.

Slocum cursed his luck, his lack of common sense trailing Joshua on foot. There hadn't been any hint the sudden rain would engulf him like this and provide an easy escape for his quarry. Would Joshua drag Beatrice along or would she be too much of a burden? If he left her on foot, Slocum might rescue her yet.

"Beatrice!"

He called her name at the same instant lightning filled the sky and thunder drowned him out. The lightning and thunder had come at the same instant, telling him the storm was directly overhead.

And the rain came down even harder. He stood and tried to get his bearings. All he could see were white slashes left by the falling rain in the night. No matter what direction he turned, rain. Which way led back to his horse proved a puzzle he could not solve.

Rather than wander aimlessly, he sought shelter. The occasional flashes of lighting illuminated the landscape, but only for a few feet. It hardly seemed possible, but the rain hammered down harder than ever.

He stumbled ahead, not sure what he might find out on a prairie that had been stripped bare by a tornado only a week before. Taking refuge in a ravine didn't seem wise in spite of the lightning crashing above his head. The gullies were getting brim full with runoff.

Miserable, lost, Slocum staggered on until he saw a low hill limned in a lightning flash. Relief lent speed to his feet. He was certain this had to be the pile of debris near the bogus campsite. It wouldn't give much protection from the storm, but he could sit on the lee side and cut the fierce wind. Although he might be soaked by the rain, he would be a little warmer since he could get away from the knifelike wind.

He approached the pile and realized this wasn't the one

at the campsite where Joshua had ambushed him. He didn't care. Any protection from the storm was welcome.

He circled, found a small spot where the rubbish blocked the wind, and sank down. The mud sucked at him, forcing him to half stand and flop backward onto the pile. For a moment, it held his weight. Then he fell backward. His arms flew up into the air as the rubble and the ground under it caved in. Slocum crashed down flat and was immediately seized by a wall of water cutting a new streambed in the prairie.

Thrashing about, he tried to right himself. The arroyo deepened and he fell farther. Lightning crackled above and he saw he had fallen into what looked like a broad, shallow riverbed. And it was all filling with water, from the distant shore to where the ground had caved in. He tried to get his balance but the roiling water spun him about. Grimly fighting, he got himself facedown in the water and began to swim, letting the current whip him along and not fighting it.

He angled toward the nearer shore, swimming hard in the powerfully raging water. A steep bank thwarted his first attempt to get free. He was tossed about, then saw a root dangling in the water. A lone mesquite had its roots exposed as the river washed away the earth under it. Making a frantic grab, he caught the rough root and snapped along as the current swept past him. He grunted, pulled himself up under the tree, and started to get free of the river.

The mesquite, roots undercut by the rain, tore free. Slocum was swept back in the river. As he was rolled over and over, his head hit a rock and his world went as dark as the Texas prairie around him.

13

Blackness engulfed Slocum. He tried to swim, but his arms had turned to lead. Calling out only filled his mouth with disagreeable, gagging substance. But with what? He tried to spit and couldn't. Not water. Sand. Gritty, choking sand. Kicking as hard as he could, he rolled onto his back and stared up at the night sky.

Occasional flashes of lightning lit the clouds, but the actual lightning bolts were nowhere to be seen. He heard the distant thunder, then realized the rain wasn't hammering at his face. The storm had moved on.

Forcing himself to sit up, he saw he had washed up on a sandbar in the middle of the raging stream. The powerful current split at his feet and worked to devour the island of safety. The runoff feeding this river had not stopped, although the rain had. When his boots caught the forceful flow, he scooted back a few feet to better avoid the water. The speed with which the water eroded the sandbar told him he didn't have much longer before being cast into the flow.

Slocum stood, gagged on the sand that had been jammed into his mouth, bent, and retched. This got some grit out. It also left a burning in his throat and mouth that caused him to puke again. When he had emptied what little he had in his belly, he took off his bandanna and wiped out his mouth. Soaking the cloth in the river and wringing it out cleaned it of vomit and sand. He retied it around his neck and then peeled his hat brim from his forehead so he could push back his Stetson to get a better look at his predicament.

The nearer bank was only a dozen feet away. In the other direction he'd have to cross more than twenty feet of river, but the way the water curled and boiled around submerged debris told him the longer distance was safer. The near bank required crossing water that might be too deep. In the other direction rocks poked up in the stream and limbs caught on underwater rubble.

He had to step away when more of the sandbar disappeared. Slocum took a deep breath, then launched himself to the far bank. The current dragged at him instantly, but he was prepared for it. He caught a rock, spun around, and floated to a tree limb. The wood gave him a few seconds' respite, then he fought his way in the watery doom and gasped when something underwater hit him in the chest. Slocum kept spinning, fighting, and an eternity later clawed at the slippery bank.

He dug in his toes, got better purchase, and heaved hard to land flat on his face. This time he didn't mind the mud trying to work its way past his lips. He got on his hands and knees, spat, and then let out a whoop of glee. He had escaped a watery death in the arroyo.

Climbing to his feet, he wiped off his face again before getting his bearings. The stars were hidden under the heavy storm clouds, but the lightning flashes gave a little light. He turned slowly and knew he had to hike back upstream to find where he had tried to capture Joshua.

As he trudged along, something more came to him. His horse had been abandoned in the midst of a torrential downpour. Slocum tried to remember how securely he had tethered the gelding. He usually made certain the reins were fastened to a tree or bush that wouldn't be uprooted easily, but he had been concentrating on Joshua's campsite.

Lit by diminishing lightning, he finally reached the campsite. The two bedraggled blankets had been swept up and caught on nearby rocks. The campfire had been washed away, and only remembering where it had been convinced Slocum this was the right place. He picked up the soggy blankets and wrung them out before tossing them over his left shoulder. His own clothing was soaked, and the wind made him shiver. The blankets helped block some of the chill.

Knowing the right direction now, he reversed his path and came to where his horse ought to be.

It took him the better part of a half hour searching to realize his worst nightmare had come true. His horse was gone. Where the paint had been tethered showed no sign that the horse had reared, broken the limb, and escaped. There wasn't any leather left on the bark to show the horse had reared and yanked itself free.

Slocum squatted by the tree trunk and pulled the blankets around him. The horse hadn't run off on its own. Slocum had to think that Joshua had stolen the horse.

"You're in big trouble now," Slocum said to the night wind. "You stole U.S. mail." The notion that Joshua was in more trouble stealing the mail than he was not killing Slocum struck him as funny, giving him the first good laugh he'd had in some time. He settled down as cold resolve filled him.

Joshua wasn't going to get away with kidnapping his sister, stealing the mail and horses—and trying to ambush John Slocum.

He pulled the blankets tighter around him, then nodded off. His dreams turned to nightmares, and he awoke to a fresh dawn as tired as when he had fallen asleep.

Stretching, he looked around and decided what he needed

to do. Finding his horse was at the top of the list. If he incidentally found Joshua, good. And he needed to find out if Beatrice had been kidnapped. He was certain that she had tried to warn him about the ambush set up at the fake campsite, but he knew nothing of what had happened back in town. She might have gone along willingly with her brother since he had seen no evidence of a struggle in the stable. If this was the way it came down, Beatrice might have called out to warn him because Joshua had decided to kill any pursuer.

Or she could be his prisoner.

Slocum shook out the blankets, considered leaving them, then slung both over his shoulder and began looking around the area for any trace of Joshua and the horses. The ground wouldn't give him any usable information. The heavy rain had erased everything, but broken limbs and other spoor might give him a trail.

It took the better part of an hour before Slocum found a twig with a scrap of cloth caught on it. He recognized the color of the material immediately. The gray matched that of the enigmatic rider who had dogged him before and probably had gunned down Bonnie Framingham. All he needed was to see if there was a tear in the rider's shirt.

He got out of the wooded area and looked across the prairie. The chance Joshua had ridden straight from this point was good, but it was only a guess. It was still the only option Slocum had. He began walking. Within an hour he found piles of horse dung, hard and rain-battered on the outside but still soft inside. Whoever had come this way had done so while it was still raining the night before.

By noon Slocum trudged to the top of a rise and looked around, hoping to catch sight of his quarry. The best he could hope for on the level prairie was three miles. From the top of the rise, another mile might come under his scrutiny. A smile came to his lips when he saw the farmhouse a couple miles off. From here he couldn't tell if it was deserted, but it well could be where Joshua had gone to ground.

Approaching would be more difficult since it was wide-open prairie a mile leading to it. If Slocum had been on horseback, he might have considered taking the rest of the day, riding in a wide circle and coming at the farmhouse from the opposite direction. That way he'd be protected from sight by scrub brush and a long, low ridge that ran off to the northwest.

He had to hope that Joshua wasn't watching his back trail. Before Slocum had gotten halfway to the house, he heard an explosion. Flames lapped upward toward the sky as fire engulfed the house. Distant shrieks reached him from the direction of the house. As tired and footsore as he was, Slocum began running the last mile.

Gasping for breath, he vaulted the wire fence and went to where a woman stood with her arms wrapped around her, staring at the fire and shaking all over.

"He shouldn't have done it. There was no cause," she said over and over.

"Who did this?"

She jumped as if he had poked her with a stick.

"Who're you?"

"I'm after the man who set that fire."

She looked at his disheveled clothing, hunting for a badge.

"You don't look like a marshal."

"Was his name Joshua?"

"Yes." She spat out the word as if it burned her tongue. "Michael and I took him in and fed him, then he robbed us and . . . and set fire to our house! We've lost everything!"

"Was he alone?"

The woman turned back to staring at the fire chewing away at the last vestiges of her home. Through the fire on the far side of the house, Slocum saw a man struggling with two buckets. He set one down and heaved the other's

contents. A bit of steam rose as the water touched the fringe
of the fire. The second bucket was similarly emptied. The
man grabbed the rope handles and turned to go back to his
well.

Slocum wasted no time skirting the fire. He felt guilty at
his appreciation for the fire. The heat dried his damp clothing and warmed him for the first time in days. But the family's loss was obvious. Hardly anything remained. The walls
collapsed into the middle of the fire, causing sparks to flut-
ter high and die in the air.

"Let me give you a hand," Slocum said.

The man's eyes widened, then narrowed as he studied
Slocum. The same thoughts flashed through his mind that
his wife had already put voice to.

"I'm not a lawman. I *am* after the man who did this
to you."

"A bounty hunter?" The man's eyes went to the worn butt
of Slocum's six-shooter.

"He has a reward on his head for horse stealing."

"He had a couple with him," the man allowed. "Thought
that was strange since he didn't have any supplies."

"What about the woman with him?"

"Wasn't no woman," the farmer said.

"Let's get to putting out the fire," Slocum said, knowing
this wasn't the right time to get real information from the
man. He grabbed the buckets and pointed. "I'll fill them,
you get halfway to the house. That'll cut down how far you
have to walk."

"Back's about to go out on me hauling water up from the
well, too."

Slocum dropped a bucket down, counting as it fell. The
well was close to twenty feet deep. That was a long way to
haul back the filled, heavy bucket. The man had done yeo-
man's work to this point. Slocum got both buckets full and
lugged them to the man, who rushed to the fire and heaved
both onto the now-smoldering ruins. He might as well have

been pissing on the fire for all the good it did. The fire was dying, not because of the man's efforts heaving water onto it but because there wasn't anything left to burn.

The two of them worked for another hour until all the embers were extinguished. Slocum was tired to the bone, but he knew the farmer and his wife were in worse shape. Their life's work had been snuffed out by a stranger.

Slocum drank from the bucket, glad the water went somewhere other than onto the fire. The farmer and his wife came up to him where he sat on the ground, leaning against the rock wall around the well.

"Mister, I want to thank you for all you done," the farmer said. He had his arm around his wife's still-shaking shoulders.

"Here," Slocum said, handing over his blankets. "You look to need these more 'n I do."

The woman took the blanket and still shivered after draping it around her slender body.

"The missus said you was after the son of a bitch—"

"Michael! Watch your language!"

He looked hard at her, then turned back to Slocum and said, "She said that son of a bitch that burned us out has a reward on his head."

"He stole three horses back in Gregory. That's a crime no matter what, but it's even worse now since half the town was wiped out by the tornado."

"We caught the edge of that storm. Saw the twister bouncing along down south of us and wondered."

"We thought we were lucky," the woman said, sniffing. "We weren't harmed none by the tornado, but then he . . . he . . . that *son of a bitch* burned us out for no reason!"

Slocum knew they had gone through hell, avoiding the tornado only to be the victims of a man whose sister claimed he was crazy as a bedbug. The thought made Slocum reflect on what he knew and what he had been told. He found it hard to accept everything Beatrice said as the Gospel truth.

Her bother had involved himself in Slocum's business more than the other way around, trailing him as he tried to deliver the mail and shooting at him.

"If you have a horse, I'll ride him down," Slocum said.

The farmer and his wife looked at Slocum. They shook their heads as if they were fastened by a rod, each moving exactly the same amount as they silently told him they didn't have anything for him.

"Did you see which way he lit out when he left?" Slocum bit his lower lip when he realized how he had asked the question.

"We fed him, then he knocked over a kerosene lamp and flicked a match into it. We couldn't do anything but get out. The flames spread too fast," the man said.

"Caught my fine lace curtains."

"Which way?" Slocum repeated gently.

Again, as one, they looked over the hill where Slocum had thought to approach from if he'd been astride a horse.

"What's in that direction? He's riding north for a reason."

"We're not that far from the main road," the farmer said. "Out there, the old Gallagher place. Miz Gallagher caught the grippe and died. Never quite sure what happened to Mr. Gallagher or the three boys and girl. Might have gone up to Mesilla. Heard Miz Gallagher say once they was from those parts."

Slocum took what little food he could get from the farmer and set off walking. The hike to the top of the hill tuckered him out after all the other traipsing along and the strenuous work putting out the fire. But he got a good view from the top and saw something that erased his exhaustion. A horse nibbled at some juicy buffalo grass not twenty yards away.

He considered how best to approach the animal. Running it down wasn't in the cards. Spooking it meant he would stay afoot for a long time. So he rummaged through the food the farmer had given him and found an apple. His belly growled and his mouth watered at the fruit he held in his hand, but he had a better use for it than sating his own hunger. Using his knife, he cut it in half and held it out.

The horse's head jerked up from the grass. Its nostrils flared as it caught the scent of the apple on the moist wind. For a moment, it stared at Slocum, then slowly came toward him. Remaining perfectly still, Slocum held out the apple. The horse edged closer, looked around and snorted, then reared, its front hooves kicking out.

Slocum might have been a statue, unmoving, waiting for the right moment to act. The horse settled down and tentatively thrust out its nose. A quick bite took the half apple from Slocum's grip. He brought up the other half and kept it just a few inches away from the spot where the horse had snatched the first half. The horse moved closer of its own accord and took the apple, allowing Slocum to put his arm around its neck. Trying to shy did it no good. Slocum's grip was strong and his need greater.

The horse tried to rear again, but this time it found a man astride its back. Slocum didn't want to try to break the horse without a saddle and bridle, but it accepted his weight and calmed down.

He rode it around a bit and then chanced dismounting to grab his pitiful bundle of food wrapped in a blanket. The horse watched him attentively, thinking it would get another apple.

"Later, maybe later," Slocum said, patting the horse's neck and using his knees to steer it onto the path he through Joshua must have taken.

Riding without a bridle was difficult but not impossible. Slocum laced his fingers through the horse's tangled mane and used this grip the best he could. The horse hadn't been on its own long enough to revert to wild mustang. If anything, it took to Slocum astride and galloped smoothly, not trying to throw him but reveling in the freedom of the run.

An hour passed and Slocum began seeing evidence of

another horse traveling this path recently. He couldn't tell if it was one horse or many. The muddy ground kept him from getting a good idea but he identified at least one other horse.

"Two," he said. Patting his horse's neck, he asked, "Were you the third one stolen from the Gregory livery?" The horse refused to answer. It enjoyed trotting along too much to bother with such speculation.

A road beckoned in late afternoon. Slocum saw spoor and tugged on his horse's mane to slow it. If allowed its head, the horse might have run the livelong day. Now was the time for caution since the road led somewhere. The twin ruts had been kept clean of weeds by frequent travel. It took all his skill to keep his horse from racing along when they rounded a bend in the road and another farmhouse appeared, set in a hollow to protect it from the incessant prairie winds. A few scrub oaks grew around it, and down by a running stream, Slocum saw a dozen cottonwoods.

More than this he saw a barn about ready to fall down because of disrepair, and through the open door poked the rear end of a horse.

Slocum recognized the paint immediately with the mail bags still slung behind the saddle.

He drew his six-gun and rode forward slowly, ready to have it out with Joshua.

14

Slocum rode around the barn and came to it so the ramshackle structure shielded his approach from the house. He
kicked free and made sure he had his few pathetic belong-
ings with him because the instant his feet touched the
ground, the horse bolted. Barely getting his fingers free of
the tangled mane, Slocum stumbled and almost fell.

He silently saluted the horse as it raced away, free of riders again. It had been a good mount, stronger and faster than
the paint, but Slocum chose the horse partly hidden in the
barn. The paint snorted and pawed at the ground as he
approached and peered through a broken plank in the side
of the barn. A huge brown eye just inches from his peered
back.

"Joshua didn't even bother unsaddling you," Slocum said
in disgust as he shifted position to get a better look past the
horse and into the barn. He considered ripping off a couple
boards and squeezing into the barn but decided that might
draw more attention than just walking around through the
main doors.

The paint nickered in greeting. Slocum regretted having

given the entire apple to the other horse, but it had been a necessary bribe. He looked around for grain or hay. The barn was bare. Moving quickly, he stowed his food and the blanket over the mail bags still strapped to the paint. Joshua had simply ridden the horse in, tied the reins to a large iron ring, and left.

Slocum tried to guess how long the horse had been stabled here. He took a few minutes to be sure the horse had water in a wooden tub before turning his full attention to the farmhouse. Like so many other structures out on the prairie, it had seen better days. The tornado had passed to the south but the huge windstorm surrounding the twister had ripped away half the roof and caused one wall to collapse. From the yard overgrown with weeds and the lack of any poultry, the farmhouse had been abandoned for some time.

Without any other information, Slocum thought this was the Gallagher place the two who had been burned out mentioned. Somehow, having a name to put on the tumbledown pile of boards made it easier for him to advance, six-gun ready for action.

Barely had he gone a quarter of the way when a rifle cocked. He spotted the barrel poking out between two planks, feinted to the right, and dived left, hitting the ground hard and rolling until he came up behind the remnants of a wagon. Both rear wheels were gone and one of the front ones canted at a crazy angle, telling him the axle had broken. Repairing it might have been too much of a chore for a man like Gallagher, who probably wanted nothing more than to be away from a place holding such ill memories.

A slug tore a hole in the rotted wood several inches above his head. Slocum pulled himself up into a tight ball, got his feet under him, and waited. He had learned that others lacked his patience—and most of them had died. Some at Slocum's hand but others were simply too antsy to bide their time and wait for the opportunity that always came.

More slugs tore holes in the wagon. He shoved his face

against the splintery side and peered through a bullet hole at the house. The rifle had disappeared, robbing him of the chance to aim a few well-placed shots where Joshua's head might be. From the number of bullets fired, Slocum thought only four rounds remained in the magazine. Joshua might reload when he wasn't firing, but Slocum had seldom seen anyone shooting at him with such presence of mind.

If Beatrice was right, her brother was crazy and would concentrate only on the problem in front of him.

Slocum chanced a quick look above to draw fire, ducking down fast and falling flat on his belly. Two more rounds were gone from the rifle's magazine. He used his elbows to pull himself along and look out. Joshua anticipated this move. A bullet kicked up dirt just inches from Slocum's nose. He flinched and a second round tore through the wagon.

He might have been wrong about the number of rounds in the magazine, and if so, he was a dead duck.

Digging his toes into the soft ground, he shot to his feet and ran for the house. He triggered two rounds intended to drive Joshua to cover rather than actually wing him. If a slug found a target in the man's belly, so much better, but Slocum saved the last four rounds in his Colt's cylinder for that.

He hit the side of the house hard, his shoulder breaking apart one of the rotted planks and sending him crashing into the house. A flash of movement. He fired. His quarry yelped and shoved a large chair toward him.

Slocum avoided it easily, stepped onto the seat of the chair, and peered down at . . . Beatrice cowering at his feet.

"John!" She dropped the rifle and sat back, hands on the floor to either side and her legs straight. "I thought it was Joshua come back for me!"

"Where is he?"

"I . . . I don't know."

He was slow to holster his six-shooter. Jumping down from his perch on the chair, he picked up the rifle and opened the breach. A cold chill passed down his spine, then disappeared as relief filled him. There had been one more round in the magazine.

"How long has he been gone?"

Beatrice scowled. Slocum wasn't asking the right questions.

"Aren't you wondering how I am? I'm fine, thank you ever so much. No, my brother did not harm me."

"He kidnapped you back in town?"

"What else?"

"Why'd he abandon you here?"

"I can't say. He doesn't reason like other men. I'm not sure he has any common sense at all but only reacts."

Slocum found himself skeptical about that. If it had been Joshua who had trailed him on his earlier mail deliveries, he was doing a whale of a lot of careful planning and not simply jumping about like a flea on a hot griddle.

"How'd you come by a rifle if you were kidnapped?"

Beatrice looked sly as she said, "I'm not without my charms. I hid it and he never bothered searching."

A derringer could be easily hidden. Maybe even a six-shooter, but a rifle? Slocum didn't press the issue.

"We should get on back to town."

"Town? No, not there. I need to be safe from Joshua. He'll find me there for sure."

"Then I can take you to Fort Stockton. You'll be safe in the middle of all those soldiers." He didn't miss the way she lit up, then tried to hide it.

"That's a good idea, John. A really good idea. When can we leave?"

He didn't see what had been keeping her by herself. If her brother had ridden away, even for a short while, she could have claimed the paint and hightailed it.

"Why'd he burn down those settlers' house?"

This caught her by surprise. She started to say something, then words failed her.

"A few miles to the east. He ate their food, then burned them out."

"He was always fascinated by fire. I didn't know anything about that."

"Thanks for warning me when he tried to ambush me at the fake campsite. He'd just have enjoyed watching the campfire and thought I'd come to it like a moth to a flame."

"I couldn't let him kill you like that."

Slocum held back a sarcastic reply. She had just come closer to ventilating him than her brother had with his careful trap. A new idea cropped up. By calling out to him at the campsite, Beatrice had guaranteed that he would try to rescue her. Had she been used as a stalking horse?

He looked around. She had a small valise. When she saw his interest, she hastily picked it up and held it close.

"He let me bring this. To keep me quiet."

Too much didn't make sense, but Slocum had reached the point of not giving a good goddamn. If Joshua had kidnapped her directly at the livery stables in Gregory, how did she have the valise since it hadn't been with her when Slocum left her? And he wasn't buying her story about hiding a rifle from a man who had kidnapped her. Even if he believed Joshua was crazy, he wasn't stupid and he had good eyes. The shot that had killed Bonnie Framingham proved that.

"You have a horse of your own or is there just the paint?"

"We can get rid of the mail bag and ride double." Beatrice wiggled all over in anticipation. "I'll like that, my arms around you as we ride. I'll see that you like it, too."

Slocum batted at something fluttering around his head. Then came another and another, this one making a loud splat on his hat brim. He looked up through the section where the storm had ripped away the roof and caught a fat raindrop in one eye.

"We'll have to ride out the storm rather than riding for the fort," he said.

"Afraid of getting wet? I enjoy it when you get me wet."
She spoke in a teasing voice but saw that Slocum was in no
mood for joshing.

He remembered too well being swept away by the cloud-
burst and how he had almost drowned in the arroyo. Risking
that again, and this time with a woman who might have been
trying to kill him, didn't set well. He lowered his face and
listened to the increasing tempo of rain against his hat brim.

"There a spot in the house where it's likely to be dry?"

"I don't think so. The roof's gone."

Slocum scooped up a tarp that was half buried under
rubble and shook it out. A few tears might let through water
but being under it was likely drier than trying to find a spot
out in the barn that didn't leak. He worried more about his
horse than he did Beatrice.

"We can make a lean-to!" The woman took the tarpaulin
and draped it over a fallen beam, then fastened the ends with
broken furniture. She pointed. "There's a mattress. Drag it
under the tarp. Hurry or it'll be soaked through."

Slocum struggled to pull it along. It had been in the earlier rain without a chance to dry out. He found another tarp
and dropped it over the mattress, then sank down as the rain
began pelting down harder. The sound of the rain hitting
the wood all around reminded him of battle, of constant
barrage. Only these bullets were watery and not leaden.

He stretched out and felt his entire body protest. Riding
bareback most of the day had taken its toll on him, yet he
was hesitant to fall asleep.

Then there was reason not to. Beatrice sidled up and
pressed close, her hand on his chest.

"Your shirt's damp," she said. She began pushing back
his coat and vest and the shirt underneath until bare skin
was revealed. She bent over and kissed him, her tongue
swirling about in the chest hair. She worked lower, down to
his belly. Tugging more insistently now, she opened his shirt
to the waist and kept kissing. Her lips touched lightly,

teasing him and causing a reaction he wanted to deny but couldn't. He was getting harder as she settled down toward his crotch with her mouth.

"Yes," she said, her breath hot as she unfastened his gun belt and then popped the buttons on his fly. She pounced on his burgeoning manhood, sucking the bulbous tip entirely into her mouth.

Slocum lay back and let her work him over orally. The rain pattering down on the tarp was as soothing as her mouth was arousing. He lifted his head enough to see the top of her head bobbing up and down as she took him ever deeper into her mouth. He groaned as his manhood slipped along the soft inside of her cheek and then lodged deep in her throat. She made gobbling sounds and slowly pulled back, letting him slip from between her lips with a wet *pop!*

"You taste so good. But I want more of you. Lots more," she said.

Slocum didn't say a word as she moved to straddle his waist. Her head brushed against the tarp but Beatrice didn't notice. She was too busy reaching down to take him in hand and guide the plum-tipped organ to her sex lips. He groaned again as she rose up, positioned herself, and settled down. Slocum couldn't see where he'd buried himself because of her full skirts but he felt it. Along every inch of his cock he felt her warmth and wetness.

When she tensed, he felt velvety pressure and heard lewd sucking sounds as her woman juices leaked down his shaft.

She closed her eyes and began rotating her hips, stirring him around within her as if he were some fleshy spoon. When she rose and fell, heat built from the friction. Slowly at first and then with more determination, she moved. Her hips began a combination of movements. Rotating and lifting and falling until he was sure she would break him off inside her.

"Oh, yes, so big, you fill me so!" She leaned forward, her

hands pressing into his chest as she continued her deliberate movements.

Then her hips exploded in a frenzy of activity. Slocum felt as if she would burn him off, break him off. But he only did the impossible. He grew harder inside her tight fleshy tunnel.

Beatrice shoved herself away and lifted her feet on either side. With an agile twist, she turned sideways while keeping him inside her. She repeated the move and faced away from him. Leaning forward, she bent him at a new and thrilling erotic angle. Then she began moving more frantically.

Slocum half sat up and reached around her hips, fumbling under the rolls of skirt, until he found bare flesh. She sobbed out when he found the tiny pink spire at the top of her sex lips and began pressing his finger into it. The slippery little spike eluded him when she lost control entirely and thrashed about atop him.

He had to lie back and concentrate on not losing control. But he fought a battle he could not win. The pressure all around, the slickness and the movement, robbed him of his spunk. He blasted forth, spilling his seed until he went limp and slid from her churning slit.

Beatrice spun back around, still straddling his waist, but this time she wasn't a wheel spinning on his fleshy axle. Kicking out her legs to press outside his, she lay down with her cheek against his bare chest.

"You are so good, John, so good. Better than anyone else. Anyone . . ." Her voice trailed off as she went to sleep. Slocum heard more in her words than she uttered.

He had expected her to say, "You're a better lover than anyone else except . . ." Who would she have named?

He didn't know and that was why he found it so difficult to trust her or anything she said. Still waters ran deep, and none were so secret as Beatrice Sampson.

15

Slocum rode, uncomfortable with the way Beatrice held him so close and pressed in from behind. The paint wasn't happy carrying two riders either, even if Beatrice wasn't that heavy. Step by slow step the horse wended its way across the drier sections of countryside, avoiding the puddles and mud holes left by the rain from the night before.

"I like this, John. I hope it never ends."

"Fort Stockton is only a day's ride off, if I have my bearings." He had worked out his location at the Gallagher farm when the stars appeared in a cloudless sky just before dawn. Whether following Joshua or trying to deliver the mail, he had ridden in a circle with the fort at the center. The best he could tell, he had never been more than fifteen miles from the fort and maybe twenty from Gregory when he had ventured south of Fort Stockton trying to deliver the package to Justin Framingham.

That thought caused bile to rise in his mouth. From the time of the stagecoach holdup to Bonnie Framingham's murder, he had locked horns with Joshua and had never come close enough to actually take the man by the throat and shake him.

"What's that, John? It's not a purr like a kitten. More like a growling dog." She moved her hands up to press into his chest. Where she touched was warm but not as warm as where she'd placed those hands a few seconds earlier. That had made riding along mighty uncomfortable.

As much as Slocum distrusted her, she had a way of making him respond that proved both arousing and irritating. He had lived his life by taking what was freely given and letting what wasn't go. Sometimes it had been necessary to take what was rightfully his, but for the most part finding a new horizon and riding for it had suited him well. He never ran from trouble, but he never sought it out either. That was too much like picking at a scab until it bled. There were plenty of ways to get new wounds.

"Just thinking of your brother."

"Why? Don't worry about him. Not right now." She fell silent, and they rode on for a few minutes before she asked, "Are you still going to stop him? I mean, get him so he can be locked up and get help?"

"Madhouses don't do much in the way of helping anyone but those outside. They take away men who would hurt others." He didn't add that a bullet to the head served the same purpose and probably gave everyone a better solution. Being locked up was as bad for him as letting a wildcat murderer ride roughshod over the prairie.

"From what you said about Joshua burning out those people, he needs to be locked away. He always had a fascination with fire. I remember as a boy he would light one match after another and watch it burn until it scorched his fingers."

Slocum listened but nothing in what she said carried a ring of truth to it. And he didn't know why.

He started to ask where she and Joshua had grown up when he saw movement along the hill to their left. The paint snorted and turned its head in that direction, too.

"What's wrong?"

"Someone on foot." He listened hard and heard a wailing that chilled his blood. "Might be hurt from the sound of that."

"No, you don't have to go. That's not Joshua."

"Not everyone out here is your brother, but damn near all of them need help."

He veered from the direction of the fort and rode slowly toward the figure struggling along, crying out piteously. As he drew nearer, he saw it was a woman in a tattered wedding gown. She paid Slocum and Beatrice no heed, walking with her head down and her arms wrapped around her as she moaned in pain. The once-white dress was ripped and hung in tatters. Lace had turned yellow, as Slocum could tell through the splotches of mud. The woman's face was covered with cuts. Squinting, he made out at least one new wound that trickled down to her shoulder and stained the fabric.

Kicking at his horse's flanks, he got the paint to something more than a walk but less than a trot. The rhythm threw him from side to side and almost unseated Beatrice. She made a sputtering sound, which Slocum ignored. His complete attention focused on the woman trudging along.

"Ma'am," he called. "Ma'am, do you need help?" He stayed back in case she hid a six-shooter in the folds of her wedding dress.

The woman turned and stared at him with wide eyes. Crazy eyes.

"You're not Keith! Where's my Keith?"

"He your husband?"

"I lost him. He lost me. Where is he?"

"Were you caught in the twister?"

"John, let her be. There's nothing she can do to help us." Beatrice slid her hands from his body and clutched at the cantle now, as if rejecting him. That was fine with Slocum.

"Ma'am, you're bleeding. You want us to get you to Fort Stockton?"

"John, no! That'll delay us far too long!"

Slocum wondered what Beatrice's hurry was. Or did she simply not want to give whatever aid they could to this woman? The hollow eyes that turned to him were haunted by ghosts only the woman could see.

"He went off. Keith went off and never came back. I have to find him."

"You from town? From Gregory?"

"No, no, that's not him. His name's Keith. Where is he?" She turned and started away, arms wrapped even tighter around her scarecrow thin body.

Slocum rode alongside, pacing her. She paid him no heed.

"What's your name, ma'am? I'm delivering mail. Might be I have something for you from Keith." That was a cruel thing to say because Slocum doubted the woman's lover would be writing. She looked to have been out on the prairie longer than since the twister had roared through.

"A letter? You have a letter for me?"

"Depends, ma'am. What's your name?"

"Amanda Zimmer," she said, looking less haunted and more hopeful. "You have a letter from Keith?"

"Keith Zimmer?" To his surprise, it was as if she suddenly deflated. The woman sank down, then wrapped her arms around herself and began her journey to heaven knew where.

Slocum thought it was a trip to hell from the way she moaned and cried.

"Wait, I—"

"John!" Beatrice grabbed his shoulder and dug her fingers in until he winced.

"What?" He turned, ready to knock her off the horse. Then he saw what had caught her attention. A lone rider had stopped a quarter mile or so away and watched. The sunlight caught the man's shirt.

"Gray," Slocum said. "That's your brother!"

"Get him. You can stop him from doing so many horrible things! Hurry!"

It proved easier said than done. The paint was close to the end of its trail and had only one speed left. That slow walk might get Slocum where he wanted to go, but it wouldn't do it fast enough to overtake Joshua.

He gave up when they reached the spot where he had first spotted the man.

"Don't stop. Go after him! We have to stop him!" Beatrice's voice turned shrill, and she tried to shake Slocum. He sat as solid as a rock.

"There's no way we can catch him," he said. Looking down, he saw the distinct tracks in the soft earth. The rain had made the earth perfect for keeping the hoofprints—until the next storm erased them. From the look of the sky, it might not be anytime soon, but the season was ripe for afternoon showers.

Slocum glanced back over his shoulder and saw that the woman in her shredded wedding dress had disappeared. Finding her again would be easier than tracking Joshua, but it seemed as pointless. Joshua would lay another ambush. Unable to do more than walk the tired old paint horse, Slocum could never escape. And why ride into a crazy man's rifle sights?

"We'll get ourselves on to Fort Stockton."

"But Joshua . . ." Beatrice subsided when Slocum turned the horse in the direction they had been heading and resumed the steady, slow trek toward the Army post.

Slocum insisted they both dismount after another hour of travel to give the horse a rest. Beatrice slid off the back of the horse with ill grace, muttering darkly to herself. If the horse had been up to it, Slocum would have galloped off and left Beatrice where she stood. They weren't far from the main road into Gregory. And beyond the town lay the fort. She could be safe and sound before sundown.

But he didn't try. The horse wasn't up to the effort of trotting off faster than Beatrice could run. He stretched, then stood in the stirrups and took a good look around.

A glint of sunlight off metal caught his attention. He reached for his six-shooter but stopped before he drew. The light reflected from something flat and was not a rifle barrel.

"What is it?"

"I don't know." Slocum looked harder and then got his bearings. He sat and simply stared. They were about three miles from the road, and he knew he had spotted his salvation.

The only trouble with that was not wanting to share it with Beatrice.

"Well, are you going to walk, too, or do you just want to torture me?"

He dismounted and walked toward the road, memorizing landmarks as he went. Long after the paint had rested from carrying its double load, Slocum remained on the ground. When they came to the double-rutted road into Gregory, he turned and looked behind.

"Is it Joshua? Has he been following us?"

"No sign of him," Slocum said, making sure he could find this section of the road easily.

Later. After he made sure Beatrice was secure at Fort Stockton.

"We can go into town or push on to the fort. I'd prefer to get to the fort."

"All right, that's suits me," she said. Hands balled on her hips, a determined look on her face, Beatrice might have been a statue dedicated to stubbornness. "I am tired of your attitude and want nothing more than to see you on your way."

"You're keeping me from delivering the mail," he said. Slocum almost laughed at that. He didn't have to deliver the mail. It would be easy enough to leave the mail with the stationmaster in town and simply ride away—to a destiny rich enough to make the tornado and its aftermath worthwhile. No matter that people had died. He knew how to make it all worth his while.

But Underwood would demand the return of the horse,

and Slocum didn't have money enough to buy another horse and gear, even with the greenbacks he had picked up back at the Gregory stable after Beatrice had been spirited away. He regretted letting the stray he had caught get away, but without a bridle it had been hard to ride and impossible to keep.

"We can ride. Mount up." Slocum stepped up into the saddle, reached down, and pulled Beatrice up behind him. As he did so, he looked along their back trail and then at the sky. Storm clouds built swiftly.

He urged the paint to as much speed as possible. He had spent too much time being wet and cold and miserable from the weather. Even sleeping in an Army barracks was preferable to huddling under a tarp with Beatrice for one more night.

A slow smile came to his lips. He ought to have enjoyed himself more, but having her making love as she had, he had kept one hand near his six-shooter, just to be sure. But sure of what? He had no idea other than he had the feeling deep in his gut that she'd lied to him. He had played enough poker to learn to read his opponents over the green felt table. Women were harder to read, but Beatrice wasn't good at lying.

But what was she lying to him about? Nothing made a great deal of sense to him. That meant his best course was to drop her into the arms of Captain Legrange, deliver the mail, dicker with Underwood for the paint, and then . . .

And then he would be done with West Texas. Almost.

The horse tired the later in the day it got. Slocum wanted to walk alongside the paint to give it a rest, yet he wanted to reach the fort, too. Rather than let the horse recuperate, he pushed on since he thought that would be faster.

"To our right. Do you see him? It's Joshua. I know it's Joshua!"

Slocum jerked around and saw a solitary rider so far away that he couldn't make out any features—or even what the man wore. It might have been a cowboy hunting for strays or someone on an innocent trip. Not everyone on the prairie had to be a crazy brother intent on doing whatever Beatrice thought he would do.

"What does he want from you?" Slocum asked. "He kidnapped you. Why?"

"He—we—he's very jealous. He doesn't want me to be with any other man."

"He's your brother," Slocum said. "What do you mean that he doesn't want you with another man?"

"That's why he gunned down my husband. He never approved of Fred. Said he wasn't good enough for me. Joshua thinks he's my father, that he ought to take care of me. He's crazy!"

Slocum got a crawly feeling in his gut that Beatrice was close to the truth—but still didn't tell him everything. That made him all the more eager to drop her off in the captain's arms.

"I can't do anything about him now," Slocum said. The rider had halted and watched their slow progress toward the fort. "Can you get the captain to send out a patrol? They can track him down mighty quick. We're not more than a mile or two away."

"Captain Legrange might do that for me," she said carefully. "Since you won't."

Slocum turned, his face clouded with anger. He came within a hair of pushing her off the horse and let the devil take the hindmost. She and her brother played some game that he couldn't figure out the rules to, and he wanted nothing more to do with them. Only his sense of honor and duty allowed her to remain on the horse. He had told her he'd see her safely to Fort Stockton. And he would.

He turned back and got the horse moving as quickly as it could go. Now and then he glanced over to the distant rider, but before Fort Stockton came into view, the rider disappeared.

"Good thing we're there," Beatrice said anxiously. "Looks like it'll be a wet night again."

Slocum grunted and said nothing. He fixed his eyes on the break in the low fence around the fort and rode straight for it. The sentry saw them coming a couple hundred yards away and had raised the alarm by the time they arrived.

"You're expected," Slocum said when he saw Captain Legrange rushing out to meet them—to greet Beatrice. He had no illusions that the post commander cared one whit about a man who couldn't even deliver the mail without getting into trouble.

"Beatrice!" Legrange pushed past the guard, who stood at port arms. "Are you well?"

"Oh, yes, Captain, I am so glad to see you again!"

She kicked free of the horse and landed hard, running to the officer. She threw herself into his arms, and he spun her around. This was hardly the greeting the captain gave everyone who came to the post, but Slocum knew they had a special relationship.

Just as he and Beatrice had had the night before. The difference lay in the affection being mutual.

"Come along, my dear. I mean, Miz Sampson." Legrange held out his arm. The woman took it.

"A moment, Captain." Beatrice came back and stared up at Slocum. "Thank you for escorting me here, sir."

Slocum touched the brim of his hat. She turned and returned to Legrange's side.

Slocum thought the storm had arrived and a bolt of lightning had released its thunder. Then he realized Legrange stiffened and sagged into Beatrice's arms. She wasn't strong enough to support him. They both collapsed to the ground.

Whirling about in the saddle, Slocum saw the muzzle flash of a second shot and jerked to the side in the same instant, his hand working on its own to draw his Colt. The bullet tore past him as he fell off the horse and landed hard on the ground. When he hit, his six-shooter went off. Then

Slocum's fingers failed to hold on to the ebony butt. Stunned by the fall, he stared up into the cloudy sky and was hit in the face with a light sprinkle that quickly changed into a downpour. As if in a dream, he was aware of men dragging him along and then fighting back weakly.

He heard someone say, "He killed the captain. Throw him in the stockade!"

"Hell, no. Let's string him up now!"

Still dazed, Slocum was pulled to his feet and shoved toward the post flagpole with a sturdy cross brace that would serve nicely as a gallows. For him.

16

Slocum felt his hands being fastened behind his back as he was shoved along. He crashed into the flagpole, shook his head clear, and looked up. A rope snaked upward and then came down on the other side to swing ominously. Soldiers stepped up to tie a noose as others held Slocum.

"What the hell's going on?" The roar echoed across the parade ground, bouncing off buildings and seeming to grow in volume.

"You stay out of this, Sarge. This jasper jist kilt the captain!"

"Like hell!" Sergeant Wilson hobbled over, leaning heavily on a cane. When the private working to tie the noose didn't stop, Wilson whacked him with the cane, driving him back. "Get away. Fall in, damn your eyes! Fall in!"

The soldiers' strict training saved Slocum. The ranks might be ragged and the men grumbling, but they lined up in a semblance of standing at attention.

"What's going on?"

Slocum turned so that he could support himself against the flagpole. The world had stopped spinning, and his eyes focused better now. He even noticed how his wrists hurt from being so savagely tied. Blood oozed out of his flesh and across his palms.

"I rode in with Beatrice Sampson and a sniper took a shot. Hit the captain."

"His gun's been fired, Sarge," said the sentry, coming over with Slocum's six-gun. He sniffed at the barrel, then handed it over to Wilson.

"That true, Slocum?"

"I hit the ground trying to avoid a second shot. Don't remember firing, but might have."

"A second shot?" Wilson had knocked out the cylinder and looked hard at the rounds. "You," he said, pinning the sentry with a hard glare. "You said a second shot was fired?"

"Well, yeah, Sarge."

"Only one's been fired. You fire your rifle? You shoot the captain?"

"Never! I was jist standin' and the lead was flyin'."

"I heard three shots," spoke up a soldier in formation.

"That squares with what Slocum said. A shot took down the captain, he drew and fell off his horse trying to avoid a second shot. His weapon discharged when he hit the ground." Wilson walked up and down the ranks, leaning heavily on his cane as he glared at each man in turn. "You dimwits would have strung up an innocent man."

"Sergeant, he—"

"Shut up!"

Even Slocum recoiled from the fury of the command. He had been a captain in the CSA and had seen his share of salty noncoms. None had ever singed his eyebrows the way Wilson's two words did.

"We are troopers in the United States Army. We are here to protect the innocent. We are not here to violate the law. Stringing a man up without a fair trial will never happen long as I'm a sergeant in this man's Army. Do I make myself clear?"

Slocum recovered and went to stand just behind Wilson.

"Who's got a knife? Free him now. And who's looking after the captain? Is he dead?" Wilson looked at the men, startled by the idea that their commander might still be alive. "You didn't even see if he was dead?"

One man broke formation and ran off.

"You didn't dismiss him," Slocum said.

"Let him go. He's the closest thing we got to a doctor right now." Wilson braced himself and fumbled out a jack-knife to saw through Slocum's bonds.

Slocum rubbed his bloody wrists, then glanced at the half-tied noose swaying in the growing wind.

"You came by just in the nick of time."

"No reason I should have had to do anything, but with these chuckle heads . . ." Wilson grunted.

"Sarge, he's still alive. I need a couple men to carry him to the infirmary." The corpsman worked to hold Beatrice back. She was covered with blood, but Slocum saw from the smears that it was Legrange's, not hers.

Wilson gestured for the corpsman and three others to do what was necessary. He looked grim when he turned to Slocum and said, "Can't hardly believe it, but that makes me in command of Fort Stockton."

"None of the other officers are back?"

"Got word of another captain being killed. Nothing about either of the lieutenants, though neither had the sense God gave a goose. Wanted to send a wire to Fort Concho and let them know, but the captain, he said there wasn't any need. Now there is. This is worse than when the Apaches were attacking 'round the clock."

"And?" Slocum heard something more in the sergeant's words.

"Storms have knocked down all the telegraph lines. I'll have to send a courier so a new officer can assume command."

"Until then, you're in charge? Nothing like a brevet," Slocum said.

"I ain't a goddamn officer. I'm a sergeant, dammit!" Wilson stared hard at Slocum. "You were in the Army?"

"Not yours," Slocum said. "There's no way you can draft me. Doubt many of your soldiers would take orders from a former Johnny Reb."

Wilson spat.

"Damned right. I wouldn't." He heaved a sigh, grabbed at his garrison cap as the wind kicked up, and then said, "Let's get out of the storm. Comes every evening, it seems."

"At least there hasn't been another tornado."

"That one did enough trouble. None of my patrols have spotted the payroll from your stage either."

"It's out there," Slocum said. He turned and looked into the increasingly stormy distance. "So's the sniper that shot Legrange."

"I can't go after him, not with a gimpy leg and bein' in charge. I'll have to send . . ." Wilson looked around, softly groaned, then yelled, "Corporal Folkes! Get your cracker ass over here on the double!"

"Yeah, Sarge?"

"Find a couple men. You're leading the patrol to find who shot the captain."

Folkes looked at Slocum, chewed on his lip a second, and finally asked in a low voice, "He goin' along?"

"I don't want to," Slocum said. "I have mail to deliver. Underwood is about ready to throw a conniption fit over none of the letters leaving the mail bags."

"I could order you to scout for Folkes."

Slocum locked eyes with the sergeant. A wry smile came to Wilson's lips, and he shook his head sadly.

"Ordering you to do anything you don't want is a fool's errand, ain't it, Slocum?"

"You might want to see to Mrs. Sampson. And I can't

say for sure, but I'd bet you five to one that her brother's the one that shot the captain."

"He got it in for Captain Legrange? Why?" Folkes asked.

"There's some things I can't figure out, and that's one of them," Slocum said. "The second shot was aimed at me. Might be, he doesn't cotton much to any man sniffing around his sister."

"That's weird," Folkes said.

"Don't hurt yourself tryin' to think too much. Get your patrol formed, Corporal. There'll be plenty of time to consider who you're after once you're on his trail."

The corporal left in a hurry. Slocum pulled up his collar against the cold rain beginning to fall. Wilson began hobbling toward a barracks set at the end of the row of officers' quarters.

"Come on along. You can see my missus and talk to the girls. They're fittin' right in."

Slocum and the sergeant walked in silence, reaching the front door just as heavier rain began hammering down hard. Every drop smashing into the roof sounded like a gunshot. Slocum stepped in and made a point of wiping his feet on a throw rug just inside the door.

"Sorry to track in mud, ma'am," Slocum said, taking off his hat when a worn-looking woman came from the kitchen and wiped her hands on her apron, dribbling flour to mix with the rain on the floor. Slocum bent to mop it up with his bandanna.

"Don't you bother none on that," she said. "You're Mr. Slocum? I recognize you from how he goes on about you."

"Sergeant Wilson?"

"That's post commandant to you, Slocum." Wilson hung up his garrison cap and shook off some of the rain like a wet dog, sending water flying all over. This brought an immediate rebuke from his wife. "Sorry, dear."

"The girls?" Slocum asked, looking past the woman to the kitchen. Audrey and Claudia pressed close together, whispering between themselves and looking up fearfully now and then. He smiled and then turned away.

"Doing as well as can be expected. But the captain refused to give us additional rations for them, so we've been splitting what we have and taking charity from others."

"He's been busy. Got too much to do to tend to minor requisition requests," Wilson said.

Slocum didn't believe it.

"I'll see what I can do. I have an in with him."

"With Legrange? Or his whore?" Wilson bit his lower lip as he said it, then looked guiltily at his wife. Whether she heard or chose to ignore the outburst hardly mattered since she didn't respond.

"Does it matter as long as you get the proper rations for the girls?"

"It costs so much to raise a family," Mrs. Wilson said. "I had forgotten how hard it could be." Then she smiled. "I don't mind. Are you staying for dinner, Mr. Slocum?"

"Got mail to deliver, ma'am," he said. Relief flooded her features even as she politely argued about him staying. "Best be on the trail right away, in spite of the weather."

Wilson held the door for him as he stepped out into the rain, then edged behind him and closed the door.

"The girls are a blessing, Slocum. Don't go meddling. That'd only rile the captain."

"Don't worry," Slocum said. "You'll do just fine. That the infirmary?" He pointed across the parade ground.

"You shouldn't go out in the storm. I'm thinking about recalling Folkes until it lets up. Weather has been a real bear this year. That twister, then all this rain."

Slocum said his good-byes and ran across the sopping field, finally glad to reach the overhang just outside the infirmary door and the protection it afforded. He ducked inside and took in the scene in a glance. Legrange was sitting up in bed, his chest bandaged. Beatrice sat close at hand. The corpsman looked uneasy even being in the same room with them.

"He'll be all right?" Slocum asked. The corpsman nodded and backed away even farther.

"Captain Legrange, you taking command of the post again?" Slocum asked.

"Again? I never relinquished it, sir!"

"While you were laid up, Sergeant Wilson took over. A good man. He deserves to be kept happy."

"What's this about?" Beatrice looked startled.

"He's got two more mouths to feed, Captain. Why not call those two little girls his by adoption?"

"We're short of rations as it is, sir," Legrange said gruffly. "We must feed our troopers first, then their families. And those two girls are not his legally. You know that."

"I know their ma and pa got killed, and the Wilsons are likely the only family they'll know till they're all growed up," Slocum said.

"No."

Slocum turned to Beatrice and said, "Might be Joshua killed their parents. He's been a real terror all over these parts." What he said was a patent lie because the girl's ma and pa had been killed by the Terwilligers, but Slocum wasn't above stretching the truth—a lot—to get help for the needy orphans. "You might try convincing the captain how it's the right thing to do, feeding those girls from post supplies."

"Joshua?" Beatrice put her hand to her mouth.

"I've got to go. Might be the patrol Sergeant Wilson ordered out will catch the sniper."

Beatrice moved her hand just enough to mouth her brother's name. Slocum couldn't think of anyone more likely to have gunned down the captain and tried to put a slug in him. With that, he left. He heard the woman arguing with the officer about feeding little children. Slocum allowed himself a small smile as he stepped into the rain. If anyone could change Legrange's mind, it had to be Beatrice. When she had started stepping out on her husband wasn't much concern to Slocum, but he didn't doubt that Beatrice had been seeing Legrange while Fred Sampson traveled about.

He frowned as he began to wonder if the stage robbery and the single shot that had killed Fred Sampson had been done by Joshua. Beatrice seemed sure it had been. For the first time, he was coming around to believing her suspicions had a kernel of truth to them.

Seeing Corporal Folkes and two soldiers riding out, slumped against the storm, made him hurry. He wanted to ride with them. Might be he could put them on the sniper's—on Joshua's—trail.

17

"If I find that varmint, maybe I kin git myself some sergeant's stripes," Folkes said. He swiped at water trickling down his face, then shook, sending droplets in all directions, forcing Slocum to look away.

"Better think on keeping to the trail," Slocum suggested. "The shots came from this direction, and he's likely to ride straight away rather than circle the fort."

"You in the war?" Folkes asked. "You got the sound of command whenever you say somethin'."

Slocum wasn't going into his time spent in the CSA. He had no good memories of combat, of the killing or the way he had almost died toward the end of the war. He certainly had no good memories of the war's aftermath and carpetbaggers trying to steal his family's farm.

"I've spent a fair amount of time tracking men."

"Bounty hunter?"

Slocum looked hard at the corporal. He wasn't inclined toward small talk, and he certainly never spoke of himself. Not to men like Folkes.

"Where'd a man take shelter against the rain?"

Folkes snorted and shook his head again, sending more water flying.

"There were a whole lot of places 'fore the twister hit. We sent out patrols and most haven't come back, in spite of it bein' more 'n a week since the countryside got all tore up. Me, I'd hightail it into town."

"Not if you didn't want to be seen—or found." Slocum considered what Joshua might do in Gregory. The man knew his sister wasn't there. It wasn't likely anyone had seen him steal the horses from the livery stable, but would Joshua know that? Would he even care? Slocum was past trying to figure out how Joshua thought.

"You figger he tried to kill the captain or that whore of his?" Folkes looked sideways at Slocum, as if worrying he might get punched out for the question.

"Can't say," Slocum said. "Might have been me he was aiming at, and he missed and got Legrange instead."

"A man like you'd have enemies," Folkes allowed, "but enough to come out in foul weather like this?"

Slocum let the comment pass. *A man like you.* What sort of man was he? He looked back at the mail bags and knew he had a job to complete. Tracking ambushers in weather like this only delayed completing the chore. Driving a stagecoach wasn't the greatest job in the world, but it was honest work. Until the company brought in a new stage, delivering mail would bring him a few needed dollars and put him astride a reliable, if ancient, horse. He patted the paint's neck and got a whinny of protest for going out in such inclement weather.

"Any farms in this direction where he might go to earth?" Slocum pointed into the drizzle. Gray clouds refused to part and let in sunlight. It had been dark so long he wasn't even sure what time of day it was. Slocum wasn't about to pull out his pocket watch to find out because it didn't matter.

They either found the sniper quick or they wouldn't find him at all.

"One or two. Cain't even find the road." Folkes looked around and held up his hand, halting the other soldiers with him. "Boys, we're goin' back. No way can we find shit in rain like this. What about you, Slocum?"

"I'll stop back by the post when I deliver some more mail."

Folkes shook his head, tugged on the reins, and got his now-eager horse moving back toward a dry stable. Slocum watched the trio vanish behind a curtain of fog dipping down amid the rain, then pushed on into the storm.

Barely a mile later the storm broke and feeble shafts of sunlight poked through the clouds. As Slocum spotted a farmhouse with a curl of smoke rising from the chimney, he also saw a figure trudging along, head down.

He decided it was better to go to the farm and guided his stalwart horse down a muddy path into the house's front yard. Chickens clucked fitfully from a nearby henhouse and a barking dog caused a man to come onto the porch. From the way he stood, he held a six-shooter at his side, ready to use it. Slocum lamented how the tornado had changed life in West Texas. Before, folks had been open to strangers and now only suspicion reigned.

"Howdy," he called. "I'm delivering mail. Mind if I get out of the wind?"

"Where's Teddy?"

"He the usual mailman? Lit out for parts unknown's what I heard," Slocum said. He detailed how he had been stage-coach driver and finally come by the mail job.

"Come on down, mister."

Slocum dismounted, led his paint to the lee side of the house, and finally pulled the mail bags free. The horse gave an almost human sigh being free of yet more weight on its hindquarters. The bag slung over his shoulder, Slocum went back to the front porch. The farmer didn't invite him inside, and he didn't ask. From behind chintz curtains poked two sets of eyes watching him.

"Your kids?"

"Are," the farmer said. "You got mail for Reynolds in there?"

"Well, sir, let me see." Slocum spread out the mail, mostly dry, and began leafing through the packets until he had a small stack for Alman Reynolds. He held them out. "This you?"

"Is," the farmer said. He snatched the letters with his left hand, then leafed through the pile using his thumb to slide the letters over one another to read the return addresses. A slow smile came to his lips, and he relaxed. "Reckon you are who you say."

"I am," Slocum said. He gathered the undelivered letters and stuffed them back into the mail bags. One was almost empty. It would be a while until he could turn both bags over and turn out nothing but dead bugs and gritty sand. "Can I ask a favor of you?"

This made the man tense again. Slocum still hadn't seen what the man held in his right hand, slightly behind his back.

"What?"

"I saw a woman walking along. Dressed in a wedding gown. She doesn't seem right in the head. You know anything about her?"

The man stepped back and thrust the letters into his house as the door opened a fraction. He tried to close the door, but a woman came out, her lips pulled into a thin slash.

"Really, Alman, the man isn't going to harm us."

"Mary, we—"

"Ma'am," Slocum said, "I understand your husband's concern. Some soldiers and I ran into a nasty gang a few days back. They'd killed the Yarrows and—"

"All of them?" Mrs. Reynolds sucked in a deep breath and held it.

"Their two girls are over at Fort Stockton."

"Do they—"

"Mary, no!"

"They've found good people to look after them," Slocum said to forestall what was likely to become a drawn-out family argument. The woman would have welcomed the two Yarrow girls into the family, and her husband likely saw nothing but trouble ahead. The tornado hadn't passed too close to them, but the incessant rain might destroy their crops and make for a difficult harvest season. More mouths to feed would push near impossible over into the deadly impossible.

"You're sure?" the woman asked.

"A sergeant and his wife lost their children. It's a good fit for all of them," Slocum said. He waited for the woman to get the upper hand in the conversation again. It didn't take but a few seconds.

"Go read the letter from your brother. He's surely sending you good news, Alman."

"Mary, I can read the letter later."

"You know the woman? It's not right she walks around looking for a dead beau," Slocum said.

"That's Miss Blaine," she said.

"Blaine? I tried to talk to her before and she said her name was Zimmer. Amanda Zimmer."

"No, she never married. Her betrothed was killed by Apaches. He was a Ranger, or so I heard in town."

"Keith Zimmer?" Slocum asked.

"Yes, that sounds about right. Poor Amanda's been wandering about for close to three years. She became unhinged when she heard about her fiancé's death over at Indian Springs. The preacher in Gregory tried to help her, but she wouldn't have anything to do with him or his congregation. She said she had to find Keith."

"Might be I can take her to Fort Stockton. There're so many people needing help, she might find it there." Slocum saw that Alman Reynolds wanted nothing more than for him to leave. His wife wanted to say something more, perhaps offer some hospitality.

"That would be good," Mrs. Reynolds said.

"I'll be on my way." When he didn't hear any argument, Slocum heaved the mail bags over his shoulder and started back into the wind. He paused at the foot of the steps leading up to the covered porch. "Other than the woman, you ever see a man wearing a gray shirt riding around the countryside? Has a rip in the shirt 'bout here." Slocum indicated a spot behind the left shoulder.

"No," Reynolds said. He silenced his wife with a stern look. From the way she held her tongue, whatever she might have said would not have helped Slocum find Joshua.

He touched the brim of his hat, loaded the mail bags back on the paint, and rode into the teeth of the rising wind. The heavy scent of rain blew into his face, but that didn't bother him much now. There wasn't any way he could get wetter than he already was.

Making his way slowly, he found a road, got his bearings, and rode away from Gregory. He didn't have a good idea where most of the people lived who were supposed to receive the mail in the bags he lugged about since the map he had gotten from Underwood only marked the farms, not who lived there, but they weren't near town. Underwood would have kept those letters to pass out himself. Slocum saw a sign with the name *Gannon* crudely lettered. He turned in the saddle and fished around inside the mail bag and found several letters that likely had to be delivered to this farmer.

He found a small trail leading away from the road and took it, but he slowed when he saw a flash of movement to his left. Trying not to be too obvious, he guided his horse around a deep mud hole to position himself properly. It took all his self-control not to gallop wildly. He saw the woman in the battered wedding gown moving as if she had been dipped in molasses, coming toward him.

Slocum watched her progress until she stopped a dozen yards away. Only then did she look up. He wasn't sure she saw him although she looked straight at him.

"Miss Blaine?"

She looked around, as if wondering where the greeting originated.

"Do you want to go see Keith?" Slocum hated himself for lying to her, but she needed to get out of the weather. If she had been wandering in this state for three years as Mrs. Reynolds had said, it was time for her to get surcease. Slocum wasn't sure anyone at Fort Stockton could help that much, but he thought her chances of finding help there was greater than in town. Even without the destruction brought by the twister, Gregory didn't seem to be as charitable as it might have been.

"Do you know where he is?" She looked around frantically. "Where is my beloved?"

"At Fort Stockton," Slocum said. "I can take you there."

"Fort Stockton," she said as if the name meant nothing to her. "Why is he there?"

"He's a Ranger, isn't he? He's helping the Army out."

"Yes, yes, he's a Ranger! You know him!"

Slocum hated himself just a bit more for the lies, but they were necessary. Her mood might change in a flash, but right now he had her willing to accompany him back to the post.

"I need to deliver some mail, but it'll only take a few minutes. Maybe a half hour. Wait for me, and I'll see that you get back to Fort Stockton."

"And Keith, my Keith!"

"Over there's a good spot to wait. Under the tree's out of rain." He looked up and didn't see any trace of lightning in the heavy clouds.

"Hurry, I've looked so long. Hurry!"

Slocum wheeled his horse about and trotted along the road to the ranch house. Cattle milled about in a feeding pen. Bales of hay had been tossed out for other animals recently.

"Mr. Gannon!" Slocum put his hands to his mouth and called again. "Got mail for you."

He knew better than to ride on up with folks so excitable after the tornado. The notion that patrols had left Fort Stockton and hadn't returned told him of widespread damage and maybe gangs of outlaws roving the country to steal what they could. The Terwilligers might have been only one of many willing to suck the lifeblood from their neighbors.

"You got somethin' fer me, youngster?" A man balancing on a cane came out and peered at Slocum. "Ride on closer so I kin git a look at you."

The man worked to polish his spectacles, but Slocum doubted clean lenses would much improve the man's vision. Milky film covered one eye, and the other was rheumy.

"These must be for you." Slocum handed down the packet of mail. Then an idea hit him. "You have any ranch hands working for you?"

"Half dozen of the laziest, orneriest varmints you ever did see. Why?"

"Might be they can deliver some of this mail and get it to the people waiting for it."

"Might be. Look at the names and tell me who you got there."

Slocum glanced over his shoulder, growing uneasy about leaving Amanda alone under the tree along the road. If she wandered off, he wouldn't have much trouble finding her. The rain had let up. The wind had turned to razors. Even if he wasn't inclined to let Amanda spend the night in the open, he didn't want to inflict that on himself when he could find a nice, dry cot in the Fort Stockton barracks.

He dismounted and spread out the remaining mail for the old man to look at. Slocum had to read the names, then Gannon nodded and made comments about those to whom the letters were addressed. Slocum learned more about them and their habits than he cared to, but when he'd finished, there were three stacks of letters.

"My foreman can take those. He's out ridin' the east fence now. Not far from the Thompson spread. He's sweet on Hank

Thompson's youngest daughter. Cain't remember her name, but she's a pistol. Cute as a bug and smart. You should see her barrel ridin'. Ain't nobody purtier. Cain't remember her name, though. But she's cute."

"What about the other letters?" Slocum began to feel trapped by the old man's insistence on going over each of the recipients.

"Both o' them's farther south. I kin deliver them myself. Need to see how they're all doin'."

"The tornado?"

"Naw, floodin'. The twister danced along to the west of here, but the hail damage was mighty awful. And then it ain't stopped rainin'."

"Thanks, Mr. Gannon." Slocum picked up the empty mail bags. Underwood would want them back. "Appreciate you having your hands—and you—deliver the rest."

"You want a nip, son? Got some mighty fine rye whiskey inside."

Slocum's throat tightened at the mention of the whiskey. But he told Gannon, "I'll take a rain check on that."

"The way the sky's been openin' up of late, you might take it *with* some rainwater." The old man chuckled at his little joke.

"When you get to town, tell Mr. Underwood you personally saw to putting those letters in the right hands."

"That old reprobate? Why, surely will, son, I'll do that. Him and me, we come out here together nigh on fifteen years ago. Gregory didn't exist then. Don't know why it does now. But I'll look Henry up and we kin talk 'bout old times."

Slocum mounted and left the rancher talking to himself about the mail going through because of his personal efforts. If it hadn't been for a sense of duty and doing his job, Slocum would have dumped the letters into a stream and to hell with it. But now that his duty was discharged, he rode as fast as the paint would allow back to the spot where he'd left the daft woman talking to herself about her lost love.

His heart jumped into his throat when he didn't see her right away. Then he heard her mumbling. Riding to the tree where he had told Amanda to wait, he was startled to see her sitting on a long branch, legs scissoring back and forth. The wind caught her skirt and whipped it about her pipe-cleaner-thin legs.

"Why'd you climb the tree?" He knew he shouldn't ask a crazy woman for reasons, but he tensed when he heard hers.

"I seen him again. I don't like him. Thought he was Keith, but he's not. He says terrible things, and I been hidin' from him a lot lately."

"Who?" Slocum licked his dried lips and asked, "A man in a gray shirt?"

Amanda's head bobbed up and down.

"Well, come on, sit behind me, and we'll go to the fort."

"To see Keith!"

The woman jumped and landed hard behind Slocum. The horse was almost driven to its knees but staggered forward enough to recover its balance.

"I'm going to see Keith. At last my love and I'll be together."

She began singing in a surprisingly clear, sweet voice. That made Slocum edgier than if she had been off-key. He rode back to Fort Stockton, eyes peeled for any sign of Joshua.

18

"Yer gettin' to be a regular in these here parts, Slocum," called the sentry. Slocum didn't recognize him, but then he hadn't bothered paying much attention to the squad that had tried to string him up the last time he rode into Fort Stockton either. "Who you got hangin' 'round yer neck this time?"

"Where's Keith? I must see him!" Amanda kicked free of the horse and ran forward.

The sentry lowered his carbine, and Slocum saw he was going to fire.

"Whoa, hold your horses," Slocum called out. "This woman's in need of some help."

"Cain't give her none without orders," the sentry said doggedly.

"Then get them." The snap of command in Slocum's tone made the soldier stiffen and almost come to attention until he realized Slocum wasn't his superior officer but was only a civilian.

"Where is he? I want to see him so we can get married!"

The sentry looked at her, then at Slocum.

"We heard 'bout this one. She's loony."

"She still needs help. Might be she can do chores around the post . . . while she's waiting for her betrothed to show up."

The sentry looked dubious, and Slocum didn't blame him much. But the soldier bellowed for the officer of the guard. Slocum wasn't too surprised to see Corporal Folkes amble up.

"You are a caution, Slocum. Never know what you'll bring in. Them kids, Miz Sampson, and now this."

"I finished handing out the mail and thought this would be my final delivery."

"Captain Legrange ain't gonna like this much."

"Ask him and see if there's not a bed for one more woman at the post."

Folkes looked sharply at Slocum, then a wry grin curled his lips. He hitched up his belt and motioned for the sentry to let the visitors pass.

"You got a wicked wit, Slocum. I'll grant you that."

With Amanda cooing to herself about finding her long-lost love, Slocum and Folkes walked slowly toward the officers' quarters.

"Slocum! Wait up!"

Slocum turned to see Sergeant Wilson making his way toward him, hardly leaning on the cane at all now.

"Where are you going with her?"

"Why, Sarge, Slocum here's takin' *her* to the captain." Folkes snickered. "Said she'd make a good replacement for the captain's bed."

Wilson lifted the cane, ready to hit Folkes, then stopped when he saw the confused expression.

"What's he talking about?" Slocum asked.

"Why'd you bring her to the post?" Wilson shot back.

"She needs help. If she wanders around too long out there, a coyote'll end up feeding on her. She needs to be watched." He sucked in his breath and looked hard at Amanda. "Might even be a soldier could see her down to the asylum outside Austin. I heard tell of a place there that takes the likes of her."

"Get the hell out of here, Folkes. And see to her. Don't you dare take her to the captain either!" Wilson waved his cane about. The color drained from the corporal's face, and he took Amanda by the arm, leading her away. "And don't let nothing happen to her, you understand?"

"I gotcha, Sarge. Nothin'll happen."

"What's wrong?" Slocum squared off to face Wilson. "I saw a woman who needed help and the Army's the only solution. You might see if the Rangers would do something to help her since her betrothed was a Ranger, but I doubt they'd much care." The run-ins Slocum'd had with Texas Rangers hadn't been pleasant, and he had not found their arrogance too appealing. For a nickel and change he would shoot the lot of them and not look back.

"Folkes made it sound as if you were bringin' the crazy lady in to replace . . ." Wilson's voice trailed off. "Oh, damn. You can't know. You were gone. Mrs. Sampson snuck off. Must have been right after you and that good for nothing corporal left to hunt for her brother."

"Beatrice is gone? Was she kidnapped?"

"Can't say she was. From the way the captain's all pissed, she must have snuck out on her own. Didn't tell him squat. Just left."

"Did she take a horse?"

"A horse and supplies. She didn't bring much with her, so there wasn't much of her own to leave with. But he's sure she left him for you."

Slocum almost laughed, then realized how it must look. He had no idea what Beatrice and Legrange had talked about. The officer had been shot up and his men had, for a time, thought Slocum had pulled the trigger. Legrange might not have been as inclined to believe the facts, especially if Beatrice said something to make him think otherwise.

But why would she? As far as Slocum could tell, the

woman was hip-deep in clover. Her husband was dead, leaving her free to marry her lover. The captain had seemed amenable to that, and when Slocum had left them, so had Beatrice. She'd hovered over the wounded man's bed like a guardian angel.

"Anything happen out of the ordinary?"

"Like what?" Wilson frowned, then said, "Wait, maybe there was something. The guard thought he saw someone sneaking onto the post and crossing the parade ground during the storm. He couldn't leave his post. I'd've skinned him alive if he had, but he didn't raise an alarm either."

"Hard to make out an intruder in the rain," Slocum said. "Especially if he's wearing a gray shirt."

"How do you know what he was wearing, if there even was anybody snuffling around?" demanded Wilson.

Slocum's mind raced. He, the corporal, and two soldiers had left Fort Stockton to hunt for Joshua, but he had simply watched them ride out, then crept into the post to find his sister.

"She might have stopped Joshua from killing Legrange," Slocum said. "That might have been the deal struck. Or he could have spirited her away."

"You're jumpin' to some big conclusions. Why can't she have just got tired of the captain and ridden off when she had a chance?"

"Where would she go? Unless I miss my guess, her house in Gregory was destroyed in the tornado. Her husband's dead, and the man she's been screwing is laid up with a bullet in him that was intended for me." Slocum stopped and thought on this a moment. "Or maybe it wasn't. The second bullet had my name on it. Her brother had a murderous bent toward any man with Beatrice. She wanted me to track him down since she believes he killed her husband."

"It wasn't a stagecoach robbery?"

Slocum had no answer for the sergeant. That looked more like the truth with every passing moment.

"If she went willingly with Joshua, it must be to keep him from killing Legrange. And if she was taken, there's no telling what he might do."

"Slocum, 'fore you came a-callin', we never had this trouble with crazy people." Wilson looked across the parade ground to the mess hall, where Folkes tried to quiet Amanda as she demanded to see her lover.

"You don't want to get too set in your ways," Slocum said, laughing. He sobered when saw Mrs. Wilson with the two girls come out with washtubs to do the laundry. Wilson followed his gaze.

"Best thing you done for us, Slocum. The utter best, but money's gettin' to be a problem." Wilson heaved a sigh. "Doesn't matter one bit. We're takin' to those girls like they were our own flesh and blood."

"They seem to be taking to your wife, too."

"Me, not so much. But that'll change when they get to know me." Wilson turned and bellowed a command across the parade ground. Two privates jumped to.

"Did the captain send out a patrol to hunt down Beatrice?" Slocum asked. Wilson shook his head and faced Slocum.

"He's worried she went off on her own, because of something he said. I heard them arguing 'fore she left."

Slocum considered this as a reason for Beatrice's sudden departure, but he thought it more likely it had to do with her brother.

"You going after her?" Wilson read the answer on Slocum's face. "Don't know if I want you to fetch her back or not. Without a decent officer corps at the post, it doesn't do to have Captain Legrange's attention all divided. Without pay for the soldiers, he needs to keep alert for mutiny." Wilson looked back where his wife and the two girls worked.

"I'm not sure I'll be back," Slocum said. "I wish you luck with your family."

Slocum shook the surprised sergeant's hand, then went

to his paint. The horse seemed in better humor without the mail bags weighing it down. Or maybe the bags flopped and made the horse uncomfortable. Whatever it was, the paint had a spring to its gait that had been lacking before. Slocum hoped that the attitude would work its way up to him.

Leaving Fort Stockton made him a bit depressed. He liked the sergeant and wished him and his wife well with the two Yarrow girls, but without the payroll, there might be big trouble brewing among the troopers. Slocum had no doubt the sergeant would defend the Army first, even if it meant shooting a few of his own men. Legrange was distracted, wounded, probably tossed into a situation over his head. Without senior officers—or even junior ones to take up the lesser chores—Legrange had a world of trouble to deal with.

Past the low wall, Slocum looked around. The rain had stopped, but the scattered clouds blocked the sun more than they let through the warmth that would evaporate the puddles and make riding easier. Still, Slocum had to do some tracking. If Beatrice rode out with Joshua, the set of double tracks might be easy to find. One set of hoofprints going in, two out. And if she left on her own accord, whatever the reason, he needed to find a single trail.

He rode in a semicircle around the main entrance and found only one horse leaving on a path at an angle to the road. If Beatrice went to rendezvous with her brother, it had to be at a place they both knew—that Joshua would use as a hideout.

The only place Slocum knew that lay in this direction was the tumbledown house where he had found her before. Joshua had been somewhere else and might have gotten angry to find his sister missing when he returned. If nothing else, the abandoned farmhouse gave Slocum a place to start. Otherwise, he had nothing.

Slocum spotted greasy plumes of black smoke struggling into the air, striving to merge with the leaden clouds above. He rode a little faster—or as fast as the paint allowed. Pushing the horse too much would only work against him if he needed to gallop. The horse had the capacity for that, but only once in a day's span. Not knowing what he would find made Slocum cautious enough to keep the horse's strength in reserve.

What had caused the fire was something Slocum didn't need to investigate, but he advanced slowly all the same. He remembered how Joshua had burned out the settlers. This was different. The family that had lived here had long since moved on, whether because of bad crops or sickness or something else was anyone's guess. The house still burned furiously.

He had to find out if Joshua had left his sister in the house.

When he had ridden to within twenty yards of the fire, his horse began dancing about, frightened of the flames. Slocum retreated, secured the horse's reins, then skirted the fire, circling the now-gutted house and going closer. He took in a deep breath, fearing what scent might be caught on the rising smoke. Slocum gagged, but it came from the stench of something that had burned within the house—and it wasn't human flesh. This didn't reassure him that Beatrice had been away when the fire started—when Joshua started it—but Slocum took it as a good sign.

As the fire died, he began poking around. He found a broken bottle with a piece of burned rag stuffed into the neck. From the way the destruction spread out from this point, the bottle had been filled with kerosene, the rag lit and then thrown against the outer wall. It broke and the part of the rag in the neck had survived to give Slocum the answer to how the fire had started.

What thrill Joshua took from the fires was a mystery, but Slocum didn't need to know why. All he wanted was to see that Beatrice was safe.

After searching another half hour, he found no sign of her or Joshua in the charred ruins. From here he widened his search and found hoofprints of two horses leading away. He might have saved himself the effort of scouring the ruins for Beatrice's body, but he knew he would have anyway. Joshua might have simply taken Beatrice's riderless horse.

He mounted and started along the trail. The clouds lifted and rain didn't threaten for the first time in what seemed forever to him. The stars slowly popping out into a black velvet sky made him feel the urge to simply find the North Star and ride for it. Instead, he kept riding south. He wasn't sure what he owed Beatrice, but letting her remain the captive of a crazy brother wasn't it.

He considered camping when twilight deepened into full night. Following the tracks required a torch, and he didn't want to announce his arrival so blatantly. And then he saw a new fire ahead. The rolling prairie dropped into a shallow depression. The house had been recently set afire because the roof collapsed as he watched. The furnace that was the farmhouse turned almost white-hot, and then the wood serving as fuel was consumed. The sudden brilliance faded as swiftly as nothing remained to feed the blaze.

Joshua wasn't far ahead.

Slocum kept the paint moving, in spite it beginning to falter from lack of rest. He crossed the half mile of prairie to the house, sat watching it turn to smoldering embers, and then heard the voices over the crackling and snapping.

"You shouldn't have done that, Bea. It wasn't right to leave me the way you did."

Slocum couldn't hear the answer but knew from the tone that Beatrice replied. He homed in on the argument and rode toward the still-standing barn. The paint whinnied in relief when he stepped down to scout on foot.

The side of the barn facing the house had peeled and blistered from the heat, but the sparks that had soared into the sky had missed the bales of hay and roof. He slipped his six-shooter from its holster and edged closer until he could hear the voices coming from inside the barn.

"You killed Fred too soon. He would have come through with the money."

"He was a crook. He wasn't any good for you."

Slocum stepped closer and saw Joshua grab Beatrice by the shoulders so he could face her squarely. Slocum wasn't above shooting the man in the back if necessary to keep Beatrice from being harmed. He sighted in on Joshua's head, then drew back, staying in the outer darkness. By the single lantern inside, he saw Joshua kiss her.

And Beatrice kissed him.

Hard. Passionately. Her hands moved over Joshua's back and down, cupping his ass and pulling him even closer.

"I'd never leave you. We have such a good thing together, Joshua."

Slocum sucked in his breath. He was beginning to understand. These two were lovers and Beatrice had married Fred Sampson to extort money from him. No one in Gregory knew much about the family because they had just moved to town. Slocum reckoned Beatrice and Joshua were drifters, hunting for men to fleece. For all he knew, they were married.

"And I give you what you can never get from any of the other men," Joshua said, beginning to unbutton Beatrice's blouse. "I set the fires for you to watch."

Slocum tensed at that. Beatrice liked watching the fires, and Joshua accommodated her. He lifted the six-gun and took aim, then lowered it. Joshua had peeled back the woman's blouse, leaving her naked to the waist. He began kissing the exposed breasts, then worked lower. Beatrice closed her eyes and reveled in the feel of his lips moving over her tits, down across her slightly domed belly, and then even lower.

Slocum stepped back into deeper shadows when Joshua lifted the woman's skirts and began exploring.

"Do you want me?" the man asked. "More than any of the others?"

"Yes, yes!"

"You should never have took up with Slocum. He was trouble."

"You shouldn't have tried to kill him. The cavalry captain either," Beatrice said, her fingers roving through the tangle of Joshua's hair. She pulled him to her crotch when he had hiked her skirts far enough.

"I hated Slocum. The captain couldn't get us anything, not after the payroll was tore off the stagecoach."

"You shouldn't have killed Fred like that. He would have got us the gold. He'd do anything I asked of him."

Joshua snorted, licked a bit at exposed female flesh, and then reared back to look up at Beatrice.

"He had his chance and didn't take it. He was getting cold feet. And I didn't like what he did with you."

"You watched?"

"Every time," Joshua said in a husky voice before applying his mouth to the woman's privates.

Slocum watched the expression on Beatrice's face. The notion Joshua had watched her making love to Fred Sampson ought to have infuriated her. If anything, it excited her. She lifted one slender leg and hooked it over Joshua's shoulder to allow him even more intimate access to her privates.

"I want more 'n your mouth," she said. "My legs are getting weak. I can't stand. Oh!"

With a swift move, Joshua stood with both of the woman's legs over his shoulders. Bent double, her crotch was lewdly exposed and pressed into his. Somehow he got his fly open. Beatrice let out a cry of pure wanton desire as he penetrated her.

Slocum stepped farther back into the night. Joshua might enjoy watching other men with Beatrice, but he didn't. Worse, Slocum had seen the woman's expression when Joshua had told her how he had witnessed every intimate moment with her husband—with Fred Sampson.

He heard the sounds of their rising passion and turned to ice inside. Joshua had tried to murder him. His guess was that the shot that had killed Bonnie Framingham wasn't intended for the woman but for him. Joshua had simply missed his target. Similarly, he hadn't made a killing shot with Legrange and had clean missed a shot that would have killed Slocum back at Fort Stockton.

He stood convicted by his own words of killing Fred Sampson.

Slocum could take him back to Fort Stockton for trial. Captain Legrange would gladly preside and then stretch Joshua's neck, but the complication presented by Beatrice might keep justice from being done. Would she intervene for her lover with the officer? Slocum thought Legrange would do about anything to get a woman as handsome as Beatrice back into his bed, especially after taking a bullet, having her nurse him and then disappear. It would be a miracle to him, and he would give her anything she wanted to return.

Clemency for Joshua wasn't something Slocum ever considered.

He heard their noisy lovemaking coming to a climax. For a few minutes there was nothing, then Joshua said, "Gotta go take a leak. Don't go anywhere."

"Never, my love, never."

Joshua came from the barn, scratching his balls and looking around. He went to the outhouse and opened the door when he realized he wasn't alone.

"That ain't my sweet Bea behind me, is it?"

"You got a six-shooter. Use it."

"Slocum?" Joshua turned slowly. He had strapped on his gun belt but hadn't bothered buttoning his fly. "You're like a wad of sap, stickin' to my boot. Can't get rid of you."

"Here's your chance. Draw. Kill me and you and your wife can go off together."

Joshua blinked in confusion, then leered.

"My wife? Hell, Bea ain't my wife."

"Your lover. It doesn't make no never mind to me what she is."

"She's my sister, like we told ever'one in town. She's my sister *and* my lover."

Joshua went for his six-gun. Whether he thought his words would shock Slocum into not reacting or he simply stated the truth didn't matter. Slocum was faster. His aim was deadly. Joshua grunted, stepped back into the outhouse, and collapsed on the wooden seat. Slocum went to him, saw he was dead, then kicked the door shut with his boot.

"Josh? What's going on? I heard a shot. You all right?"

Slocum saw a still-naked Beatrice in the barn door, the light from within turning her into a beguiling, sexy figure. A demon. Someone so evil it made Slocum shiver with anger.

"I'm all right," Slocum called out. His voice was choked and came out in a hardly more than a husky whisper.

"I'm waiting for you. Don't be long." Beatrice giggled like a schoolgirl. "You can be long. Just don't keep me waiting!"

She went back into the barn to wait for her brother.

Slocum rode his paint away, heading for town. He had unfinished business there.

19

Slocum sat astride the paint, staring at the front door of the stagecoach office. Underwood rumbled about inside, shouting at someone and occasionally throwing around paper. The shower of white caught on the wind and blew into the street. After a large gust of paper, a young boy rushed out, dropped to his knees in the road, and frantically grabbed for the paper.

Henry Underwood came out, waving around a handful of other papers.

"Get the lot of them. We can't make this business run right without—" He cut off his tirade when he spotted Slocum. The boy continued grabbing the dirty papers and clutching them to his chest.

"I got 'em, Mr. Underwood. All of them!"

"Put them into order," Underwood said, flinging down the papers he held.

"But I can't read." The boy looked stricken at the order. A new zephyr stirred the papers Underwood had dropped, scattering them and sending the boy scurrying after them as they blew down the street. "I'll fetch 'em all. I will, Mr. Underwood!"

The stationmaster came out into the middle of the street, put his thumbs in the armholes of his vest, and puffed up his chest. All he succeeded in doing was sticking his paunch out rather than looking tough.

"You finish with the mail delivery, Slocum?"

"Did."

"Then get off that horse. It belongs to the company. I got other work for you. The twister tore up some planks out of the back wall, and you got the look of a man who can swing a hammer."

"I can do that," Slocum said. He made no effort to dismount.

"Then get to it, if you want to be paid. The whole town's rebuilding. We have to be ready when Butterfield sends a new coach."

"I've been thinking on that," Slocum said. "They'd drive it out, wouldn't they?"

"Of course they would. What are you, a dimwit?"

"A driver drives it out," Slocum went on. "Why'd you want a second driver?" Slocum saw the stationmaster's face turn livid. Underwood didn't like having his schemes thwarted. Slocum would have worked his fingers off until the stagecoach arrived with the driver who replaced him.

"Get out of here, Slocum. You're fired."

Slocum pursed his lips and nodded slowly.

"Sounds fair. Any chance you'd hire me back?"

"Not until hell freezes over!"

"How much is the reward for returning the Fort Stockton payroll?"

Underwood blinked, started to say something, and looked like a fish washed up on a riverbank. He clamped his mouth shut to keep from embarrassing himself further.

"What makes you think there's a reward?" Underwood swallowed hard.

"Just asking. Reckon I'd better leave now."

"Wait, Slocum, wait! You know where the payroll is? Where is it?"

Slocum let the stationmaster stew for a few seconds. He read every thought that flashed through Underwood's skull. If Slocum still worked for the company, retrieving the payroll wouldn't gain any reward—he would be an employee and expected to return it. But being fired as he had, Slocum could dangle the promise of the gold in front of Underwood. If there wasn't a reward, Slocum could simply leave and the payroll would be lost. But a reward had to come out of the depot's operating profits.

"If you know where it is and think you're going to steal it, I'll see you in jail! You won't steal the U.S. Army payroll!"

"Never entered my mind," Slocum lied. "I just asked about a reward."

"You hid the payroll. You stole it and now you're trying to ransom it back!"

Slocum shook his head in denial.

"Who are you going to get to arrest me? The marshal's long gone. Heard tell the sheriff is, too."

"The soldiers. I'll get them to arrest you!"

"Captain Legrange owes his life to me," Slocum said, stretching the truth to the breaking point. "The other officers are still on patrol. Somewhere."

"What do you want, Slocum?"

"A reward. How big was the payroll?"

"You don't know?"

"I was only the driver, and the twister broke the stagecoach to splinters and almost took me with it. How could I know?"

"If you don't know where the payroll is—"

"I think it's time to get some supper. My belly's growling because I've been on the trail delivering the mail for so long."

He slid his leg over the saddle horn and dropped to the ground. The paint snorted and turned a large brown, accusing eye at him, as if the horse understood what he did to the stationmaster.

"A hundred dollars," Underwood said hastily, grabbing Slocum's arm and restraining him.

"That's not a very big payroll."

"That's the reward!" Underwood almost screamed.

"That's not a very big reward," Slocum corrected. "Five hundred dollars would be more in keeping with the size of the fort's payroll."

He knew he had set the amount too low when Underwood swallowed hard, then bobbed his head up and down.

"Where's the payroll?"

"A long way off," Slocum said, looking down the main street. "If I have to walk, that is. Now if I had a horse like this here paint, we could fetch the iron box with the payroll in a few hours."

"Five hundred dollars and the swaybacked horse," Underwood said. "You're a thief, Slocum, an unrepentant crook! And if you're lying about the payroll, I swear I'll see you in jail if I have to fetch a Ranger and lead him back here by the nose!"

"You'll need a good-sized wagon," Slocum said. "Either that or the key to the strongbox." Underwood muttered to himself. "I'll be in the restaurant getting some food. When you're ready, you can find me there."

Slocum put his dinner on Underwood's tab.

"This is a long way from where the stage got tore up," Underwood complained. He sweat like a pig as he fought the double-horse team across the prairie.

"It is," Slocum agreed. He stood in the stirrups and looked west. This was the trail he had ridden earlier when he spotted the flash of sunlight off metal. A slow smile came when he saw the same bright flash.

Not waiting for Underwood, Slocum cut across the gently

rolling grassland and was on the ground, brushing off dirt from the large brass plate in a thrice. By the time Underwood drove up, Slocum had revealed the iron strongbox. The lock was twisted, but the heavy plate was unscathed. Whatever had been in the box when Slocum had driven out on the stagecoach run had to still be inside.

"That's it, that's it!" Underwood was beside himself getting down to touch the strongbox as if it were a religious relic. He looked up at Slocum. "You earned the reward. If the gold's inside, that is. If it's here."

For a moment, Slocum thought the stationmaster was going to hug the box.

"Open it and see."

"I can't get it open," Underwood said. He had fumbled out a large iron key but the lock was too damaged to even insert the key.

"Stand back."

Underwood scrambled away as Slocum drew his six-shooter and fired. The first bullet careened off the lock, leaving a bright scratch. It took two more shots to break the hasp. Slocum made no move to open the box. He left that to Underwood. The man looked uneasy, even when Slocum holstered his Colt.

Then he grabbed the broken lock and threw it aside. The hinges creaked open. Underwood heaved a deep sigh as he looked at the leather bags inside.

"It's here. You found it." Underwood straightened, then said, "As you should have since you were the one who lost the payroll. You were—"

"Why take this back to town?" Slocum asked. Underwood went pale. "Let's load the payroll into your wagon and take it straight to Captain Legrange."

"You—you're—"

"Pay me the reward out of the gold. That's twenty-five of those twenty-dollar gold pieces."

"But that'd be shorting the Army and—" Underwood

swallowed hard when he saw how Slocum stared at him. He picked up one leather bag and carefully counted out the coins. It took him another minute to verify his first count.

Slocum thought he would have to pry the double eagles from the man's hand. He tucked them into his vest pocket.

"You need help getting those bags into the wagon?"

"I can do it by myself," Underwood said.

Slocum mounted and watched the man load the heavy leather bags into the rear of the wagon. As Underwood climbed into the driver's seat, Slocum tugged on his paint's reins and got the horse walking slowly southward toward Fort Stockton.

The low wall around Fort Stockton came into view. The road had dried out quickly, and a small dust cloud kicked up behind Underwood's wagon burdened as it was with the payroll gold.

"You can take it to Captain Legrange," Slocum said.

"What's that?" Underwood's startled expression said it all. "You don't want to be there, too?"

"No need. You work for the stage company. I don't any longer."

Underwood looked at the paint and shook his head, as if silently wondering why Slocum hadn't asked for more. The five hundred dollars in gold rode easy in his vest pocket, making a small bulge. That much money would keep him in clover for a long time.

"Whatever you say. I can do with some good feelings from the post commander. Legrange wasn't too happy with you losing the payroll the way you did."

Slocum started to bristle at the insult, then subsided. He had done all he could. Let Underwood have his moment in the sun. It no longer mattered to Slocum. Joshua was dead, and he had no idea if Beatrice had returned to Legrange's bed. If she didn't know who had shot her brother—her lover—she might keep on riding. Slocum hoped she didn't burn out any more farmers just to watch the flames. She was dangerous, crazy dangerous. Without her brother, there was no telling what she would do.

And Slocum wanted someone else to deal with that problem.

"Halt! What you got there, Mr. Underwood?" called the sentry.

"Got to see your commander right away. Everyone on the post is going to share in this." Underwood hesitated, then could no longer contain the news. "I got your payroll!"

Slocum had seen rumors spread on Army forts before. Before Underwood had driven through the gate, soldiers came flocking to surround the wagon, many wanting to jump into the bed and others simply content with running alongside. Underwood basked in the approval beamed his way by the soldiers.

Slocum didn't even get a moment's notice as he rode behind the wagon, then cut to the side, letting the soldiers crowd around Underwood as he stepped down from the wagon in front of Legrange's office. The officer came out and braced himself against a porch post. Slocum waited long enough to see if Beatrice joined him. When she didn't, he knew the woman had lit out for parts unknown.

He rode slowly around to the enlisted men's quarters. Mrs. Wilson was outside beating a rug. Clouds of dust billowed. She stopped when Slocum dismounted and came over, leading his horse.

"You want my husband, Mr. Slocum? He ran over to the parade ground with the others. Not sure what the fuss is, but it must be good. Every last one of them is grinning like a fool." She wiped her dirty hands off on her apron. "Can I get you some water? You look parched."

"That'd be mighty fine, ma'am." When she left to fetch the dipper, Slocum took off his bandanna, fished in his vest pocket for the reward money, and wrapped it up, tying the cloth securely into a pouch.

"Here you are." Mrs. Wilson handed him the tin dipper. Slocum drained it, then handed it back.

"How are the girls doing?"

"As good as can be expected. Losing their ma and pa like they did isn't easy, but they're getting used to Army life."

"Glad to hear that," Slocum said. "Here's something for them. You can figure out how best to use it." He handed her his bandanna with the tight knot around the gold coins.

"That's right thoughty of you, Mr. Slocum." She hefted the coins, then looked at him. He had mounted. "You want to wait for—"

"Tell your husband or not, as you see fit. Ma'am." He touched the brim of his Stetson. The two girls peeped out of the window and ducked back, as if being seen was wrong.

"Wait, Mr. Slocum." She fumbled to get the knot untied. "Mr. Slocum!"

He rode away without a look back. Nothing much good had come out of the tornado and all the damage it had done, but this went toward mending some of the woes.

John Slocum felt damned good as he left Fort Stockton and turned his paint's face northward. There might be decent work to be had in the Panhandle. And if there wasn't, Colorado had always been generous to a drifter like him.

Watch for

SLOCUM AND THE DIAMOND CITY AFFAIR

405th novel in the exciting SLOCUM series
from Jove

Coming in November!

DON'T MISS A YEAR OF

Slocum Giant
by
Jake Logan

Slocum Giant 2004:
Slocum in the Secret
Service

Slocum Giant 2005:
Slocum and the Larcenous
Lady

Slocum Giant 2006:
Slocum and the Hanging
Horse

Slocum Giant 2007:
Slocum and the Celestial
Bones

Slocum Giant 2008:
Slocum and the Town
Killers

Slocum Giant 2009:
Slocum's Great
Race

Slocum Giant 2010:
Slocum Along
Rotten Row

penguin.com/actionwesterns

M457AS0510

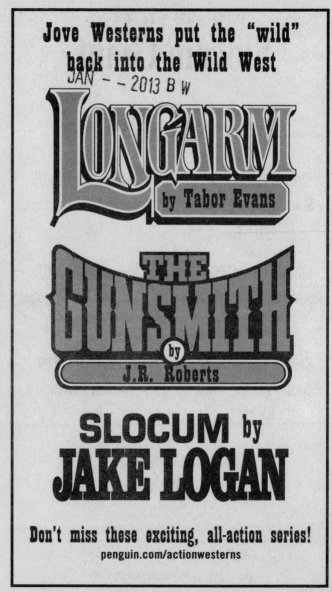

Jove Westerns put the "wild"
back into the Wild West

JAN – – 2013 B W

LONGARM
by Tabor Evans

THE GUNSMITH
by J.R. Roberts

SLOCUM by JAKE LOGAN

Don't miss these exciting, all-action series!

penguin.com/actionwesterns

M11G0610